REBEL MATE

INTERSTELLAR BRIDES® PROGRAM: BOOK 20

GRACE GOODWIN

GET A FREE BOOK!

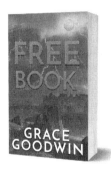

FIND YOUR INTERSTELLAR MATCH!

YOUR mate is out there. Take the test today and discover your perfect match. Are you ready for a sexy alien mate (or two)?

VOLUNTEER NOW!

interstellarbridesprogram.com

ara Novak, Transport Room, Planet Trion

I BLINKED. Then again. My eyes couldn't be working correctly because I had nipple rings. Just a few seconds ago, or a few light years away, I'd been in a drab hospital-style gown. The last thing I remembered was the warden counting down... three... two... one, and I definitely hadn't had nipple rings then. Sure, I'd had a needle jammed into the side of my head for a voice translator, but I'd have remembered having my nips poked.

When the warden had said I was to arrive on Trion prepared for the planet's customs, this wasn't what I'd expected. I knew it to be an arid place. Hot. Desert-like. Maybe I'd be in a ridiculous outfit from *I Dream of Jeannie* with billowy pants and bare midriff. Me, in harem pants. As if.

Instead, I was just... bare.

Naked.

I was lying on a small platform, the surface hard and unforgiving. Curled on my side, I looked down at myself. At the little gold hoops that went through my nipples.

I was transfixed. While it wasn't something I'd ever imagined doing, I had to admit, they looked pretty good. They went pretty well with my navel piercing.

"Thank the gods, you're awake."

The male voice had me startling and looking up. A guy came up the few steps to reach me with a garment that looked much like a robe in his hands. I pushed up to sitting, and he wrapped it around my shoulders, covering me. I couldn't miss the way his gaze raked over my bare flesh before it was hidden.

Again, I blinked.

"I am Naron, your mate. You have transported far and just for me. I have been given the ultimate reward."

When he squatted beside me, our eyes were at the same level. His were a piercing green. I couldn't miss the pleased look on his face. Bright eyes, a broad smile. Curious. Eager. Like a well-muscled, broad shouldered puppy.

"Hey," I said, then cleared my throat. The air was warm, the robe a cool silk. I glanced about. We were in some kind of primitive building with cloth walls. A large tent, like one used as a rental for parties. The material was a sturdy canvas, but a rustic brown, as if it were woven from natural materials. Unbleached.

"You are well, *gara*?" he asked, his gaze raking over me. "Do you need me to send for a doctor or are you recovered enough from transport to await the examination?"

Examination? I didn't know what that involved, so I just said, "I'm well."

I was. I still felt the tingly pleasure from the orgasm I'd gotten during the testing. God, it had been intense. Powerful. I'd even screamed as I'd awoken. But it hadn't been real, yet I felt it still. But the guy in front of me? He was *very* real.

He exhaled and gave me a relieved smile. "That is excellent news. When word was given that I was matched, I was on duty. I am relieved I was able to meet you upon your arrival. I didn't desire for you to be frightened or alone. Due to our remote location, this station is unmanned unless transport out is required." His eyes continued to shift, taking in my hair, my features. Every inch of me he could see. "I have heard that Earth females are unusual in appearance, but I find you... lovely."

I didn't know what that meant or if Trion females looked much different from me, but he didn't seem to be insulting. The opposite. I seemed to surprise him.

His eyes widened. "I do not even know your name, mate."

Mate. He was matched to me. This guy. This Trion alien.

"Zara."

He repeated it, then again as he held out his hand. I took it, and he helped me to my feet as I held the robe closed. He eyed me, perhaps ensuring I wouldn't pass out. I was tired, and I had a head rush standing up, but otherwise, I felt fine. Even my nipples which should have hurt after being pierced didn't ache.

"I am a sentinel guard to Councilor Bertok. A true

honor and position. Now I have you. I am a lucky male." He wore brown pants with a long-sleeved shirt that did look quite like a uniform. Black striped epaulets were on his shoulders, and he had a—was that a sword?—at his hip. "Ah, here is the region's leader now." He leaned close to whisper in my ear. "Females remain silent in his presence."

An older man entered the tent. I took in his long robes and regal bearing. Naron bowed, and I only stared, stuck on what my mate just said. *Females remain silent...* What the hell?

What kind of planet had I landed on? Naked? Nipple rings? Silent females?

I was thankful for Naron's thoughtfulness regarding the robe because the old guy stared. And stared some more. Not in a friendly or warm way. Nope. I felt a little creeped out. While Naron was a stranger to me, he was my mate. He would see me naked...while awake and probably soon. I didn't have any illusions that he would court or woo me prior to getting me beneath him. Yet I didn't wish to reveal myself to the entire planet, especially if this guy was his boss. Especially if this guy gave me the willies.

The man... guy, alien, was old. I couldn't guess his age but definitely older than Naron. He could be his father. Even grandfather. His hair was gray, and his face was heavily lined, but his spine was ramrod straight. I couldn't guess to his physique beneath the long robe he wore. He had an assessing gaze. It wasn't sexual as much as... predatory. As if he saw something he wanted.

That wasn't happening. I recognized that look from men before. It never meant anything good.

"Naron, word has quickly spread that you were matched and to an Earth bride." His voice was deep and imposing, laced with coldness.

"Yes, Councilor," Naron replied, setting a hand upon my shoulder. His touch was warm and reassuring.

The ice blue gaze of the older man settled on the action. "I had to see for myself your prize... a proud fighter such as yourself has earned."

I wasn't sure how I felt being a prize. I was just a woman from Boston who'd seen and done enough shit on Earth to try a hand at space. The testing said I'd been matched to Trion. How living in bitter cold for half the year made me a good match for a desert planet, I had no idea. And Naron, well, he seemed... sweet. I wasn't sweet. Far from it. Like the song, I was bad to the bone.

He appeared kind though, and that was a good start. He wasn't hard on the eyes either. At the words of praise, I saw Naron's chest puff up.

Bertok looked me over as if I were a blue-ribbon heifer at the county fair. "It's obvious you are human. Your diminutive size is that of High Councilor Tark's mate."

I had no idea who that was or his mate. I was just over five-feet tall, so I had to assume the guy's Earth bride was petite, too. Opening my mouth to respond, I remembered Naron's whispered words and closed my mouth. I had no clue what the deal was here, and I didn't want to blow it this early in the game.

Bertok stepped closer, his long robes swirling about his ankles

He stood before us, his gaze on me. I didn't know what to do other than to keep my trap shut. I knew nothing about Trion. Nothing about their ways. Nothing about—

Bertok lifted his hand, a dagger within his grip catching my eye. I barely had time to gasp before he struck. If I thought him weak and frail, his ability to slash through Naron's throat with one well-aimed slice proved I was wrong. So very wrong.

Naron's hands went to his neck, and his eyes widened in stunned agony.

"Holy fuck," I said, taking an instinctive step back.

Blood spurted onto me, hot and thick as my mate collapsed to his knees. Bertok retreated as Naron fell to the ground with a heavy thud. Dead. Very, very dead.

Blood continued to seep from his neck and into the packed dirt.

I'd seen bad shit in my time. Bad things done by bad people. Hell, I'd *done* a bunch of that bad shit myself. I was hardened from it. Jaded. Definitely untrusting. But this? What Bertok just did with ruthless precision? He wasn't even breathing hard. Hell, other than the blood on the knife, he didn't have a drop on him.

I took a step back. Then another. I did *not* want to be next. I had to get away. How, I had no idea. All I'd seen of Trion was inside this tent. Hell, I'd only been on the planet less than five minutes. I tried to hop back on the transport pad, hoping it would *Star Trek* me back to Earth. I'd tell the warden I wanted my fucking money back. Not that I paid any.

"Oh no, female," Bertok said, his voice low and menacing as he grabbed hold of my arm. "You're mine now."

His? Yeah, no. I slipped on one of the steps and stumbled to stand beside him.

Bile rose in my throat at the thought. Um... what the hell was happening?

"I... I—"

I didn't know what to say. I was numb. Afraid. So very lost and completely out of my element. It was one thing to be in a back alley in Southie dealing with shit. I'd have on shitkicker boots with jeans that had pockets for a switchblade. A cell phone. Here? Now? I was barefoot. Naked except for a thin robe and weaponless. The guy might have been old, but I was no match for that blade or his skill in using it.

"You saw what I did to your mate," he said. "I can do that to you before you utter a scream."

I took a breath, smelled the metallic tang of blood. My mate's. Wait. *Wait.*

Why had he killed Naron? He wasn't just some crazed lunatic on a killing spree. We weren't standing in the middle of a gang fight. At least I didn't think we were. This guy was sane. Focused. He had a reason for wanting Naron dead.

Me. He wanted *me.*

"You won't kill me," I replied, licking my suddenly dry lips. "You want me for yourself."

He didn't smile, but he laughed. "I do not want you for myself. I have a worthless mate already. You are too valuable to keep."

Oh shit. This was not good. Were assholes the same everywhere in the universe? This guy was going to... sell me?

"What... what are you saying?" I asked then

7

swallowed hard. I wanted to hear it from him. To know exactly what the fuck he was doing.

"Enough. Females do not speak." He reached out and grabbed my arm, his fingers like talons in my skin, and pulled me out of the tent into the bright sunshine. I squinted as I held my robe closed, trying not to trip on the long hem. We were in some kind of encampment, perhaps fifteen or twenty similar tents spread out over the desert. I saw no one nearby, only in the distance. I didn't dare scream, for they were too far to save me if this guy... Bertok, decided to use his knife on me. I tripped over the root of a scrubby bush. There were also wind-bent trees and rugged mountains in the distance, completely different from inner city Boston. Not a speck of concrete anywhere. Beyond this small clump of civilization, I saw nothing as far as I could see.

The test was supposed to offer me an almost perfect match, and it said Trion? The machine had definitely been broken because I didn't even like the beach. What the fuck had I gotten myself into? I'd gotten in and out of shit in my time. This, though, was out of my league. Or universe.

He tugged me to another tent. This one obviously belonged to him, for the floors were covered in thick carpets. Pillows and low tables with gilded bowls of fruit and other strange foods upon them. It was exotic... rich. As if this guy would skimp or live without luxuries.

Yanking my arm, he pushed me forward, grabbing the robe as he did so. It slipped from my shoulders, and he let it fall to the floor at his feet. I was naked while he was clothed.

I was fine with my body. I had no real issues with

modesty. Sure, I'd been told my boobs were small, but whatever. At least I didn't give myself two black eyes if I ran. This felt different though. Subjugation. We weren't equals, and he was making that very obvious.

"If you're selling me, rape won't make me more valuable." I began to shiver, even though it was quite warm. I tipped my chin up. I'd never let anyone see me afraid, and I wasn't going to start now. I'd never let him see how I really felt. No fucking way.

His white brow rose. "A mouthy female. I'm sure your buyer will enjoy taming you."

He turned from me and went to a table, picked up a gold chain and what looked like a thick, golden collar. He still held the dagger in his other hand, reminding me as he approached that I was definitely at his mercy. I'd learned long ago fighting back was important but to do it at the right time to stay alive. Now wasn't the time.

"Kneel."

I looked up at him, said nothing.

He lifted the knife to my neck, pressed the tip into the skin until the blade bit into my flesh.

Holding my breath, I reached out and grabbed hold of the tent pole beside me, carefully dropped to my knees, careful lest I slash my own throat. Once on my knees, the idea of giving him a BJ made bile rise into my throat. I would definitely throw up if forced.

Reaching out, he set the knife down on a table without taking his eyes from me, telling me without words it was close enough for him to grab. To kill.

With his hands free, he brought the collar forward and locked it around my neck as if I were a dog. I even had a tag, a heavy medallion hung cold and heavy on my chest. He then affixed the chain he carried to one of my nipple rings. I flinched, but he seemed to have no sexual interest in me. His hand moved to the other, affixing the chain to both, however he did so with the tent pole in between. My breaths quivered with my breasts, the chain swinging once he let it go. It was light and dangled only a few inches but... I. Was. Trapped. By. My. Own. Nipples.

What the fuck?

If I tugged, the rings would rip right out. That wasn't going to happen. The thought alone made my nipples harden. God.

I looked up at Bertok who loomed. "Just as a female should be. Naked. On her knees. Restrained."

I wasn't liking Trion all that much. How could I have been in Florida at the Brides Testing Center only a short time ago, and now, I had a dead mate and was a prisoner of a creepy old murderer who planned to sell me?

Had I been sent to Hell instead?

"You're an asshole," I muttered.

If he'd wanted me dead, my blood would be spilled beside Naron's. He needed me alive and obviously unharmed. He didn't want to rape me. He didn't even seem overly interested in my body. Based on his words, Trion females were naked, and this kind of weird chaining thing was... normal. Kinky in some situations, but this wasn't one of them.

Yeah, the testing was so fucking wrong. I had perpetual shitty luck, and it had continued into space. Wait. The match may have been just fine. Naron had been my match not this guy. Bertok was just an evil dick. But sand? Desert? Sooo not me.

"Rest." He walked toward the tent's entrance. "We

travel to Sector Zero as soon as you are strong enough to transport again. You have a delivery to make, and you won't do me any good if you're dead."

I remembered something the warden had said after my test, that once a bride accepted the match, she is no longer a resident of Earth but of the matched planet. I could never return to Earth. I just had to wonder if this was what she had in mind.

2

*I*saak, *Sector Zero, Planet Occeron, Abandoned Prillon Outpost known as* Omega Dome

"*There's a human female, just arrived.*"

"*An Earthling.*"

"*Too weak for me, one fuck would kill her...*"

"*...she's not for sale, fool.*"

"*Everything is for sale, for the right price.*"

A very large male, possibly a Prillon and Atlan hybrid with a dark-red arm band pushed his way between the chatting outlaws. "She belongs to Cerberus."

The voices carried from the back of the small, filthy room where I sat with my tech buyer. My ears had picked up on the words, the important ones. A human female was here?

I'd never known that to occur in all the time I'd been doing business here. I flicked a gaze to Ulza, for she wore the armband of Cerberus. She would know the truth of the gossip.

"It is true." She sat across from me, smirked because she knew exactly what I was thinking. "A human female in Sector Zero. But they are wrong on one thing. She is not for sale at any price. She now belongs to Cerberus."

I gave a grunt of reply, showing her complete indifference. Hopefully.

I looked down at the tech unit in my hand, confirming that she had kept her word, and the credit transfer for the latest batch of Hive implants was complete.

"You will keep your nose out of Cerberus business, won't you Isaak?"

"Not interested." Not only did I not want to become tangled up in Cerberus business, but anything involving Ulza from Cerberus? She was more dangerous than anyone else I knew. Killing Hive and selling them for parts? No problem. But even I had some honor left. And if Ulza's words were true and the female in question was here in the outer reaches of Coalition-controlled space because of Cerberus?

She'd gotten mixed up in serious stuff. The question was how?

No. I had to stay focused on why I was here. Sticking one's nose in other people's business was a good way to die.

"Are you sure, Isaak? I wouldn't want to have to kill you."

"I'm sure."

"I paid you as agreed. Now, I have business with Jirghogis."

I looked up then, the deadly blue Cerberus female watching me over the top of her drink. I knew I should keep my *farking* mouth shut, but I wasn't an outcast because I always did the smart thing. The right thing? Usually. But the smartest? No. Seems I hadn't learned a damn thing.

"Exactly what kind of business?"

She tapped her armband. I was shocked to receive an answer. "I am to deliver the human to Cerberus myself."

Her cackle made me sick. For the past five years, ever since I'd begun trading in stolen Hive tech, Ulza and I stayed out of each other's way... outside of our tech dealings. I had no desire for that situation to change. She was a cousin to Cerberus himself, was a member of Cerberus legion and a known associate of the Silver Scions, a tightly knit syndicate of doctors, engineers, scientists and killers from every sector of the galaxy. They bought Hive integration technology and sold what they could on the black market as surgical enhancements to anyone with the credits to pay for it.

Ulza bought every piece of Hive tech I brought to her without complaint. I didn't like her, but I liked her business model. She always paid, up front and on time, and never asked where I procured my goods.

"And Jirghogis procured her from...?" I asked although I knew she wouldn't answer this one. I pushed my beverage container across the scarred tabletop. The thought of any human—*fark* that, anyone at all—dealing with Jirghogis, the creature whose shipment warehouse was used for illegal trade and auctions, made me choke down bile. He was far from humanoid, a hideous creature with huge eyes and a tail thicker than my torso. His exoskeleton was covered in scales, and those scales? Coated in poisonous slime that emitted an odor designed to sear the lungs of anyone who got too close.

"So you are interested in the female." She tipped her head to the others at tables nearby. "Like everyone else under this dome."

"Simply curious. We don't get many humans out here," I replied, glancing toward the nearest exit. It was time to leave. I had no desire to investigate the appearance of an unknown human nor in why Cerberus wanted her. The last time I'd tried to save someone, my brother, Malik, had paid the ultimate price for my failure. The accident was five years past. The memory of him dying in my arms so vivid, it could have been five hours ago.

The wrong Councilor's son had died that day. Malik had bled out in my arms in the middle of the desert, and there hadn't been one *farking* thing I could do to save him. My father lost his heir, the responsible son, the one groomed from birth to take his place, and had been left with me.

Rebellious. Impulsive. Bored with politics. Lacking in both patience and diplomacy. My brother had been mere minutes older than me, but his spirit had been wise. Measured. Compassionate.

Everything I was not.

Memories of my brother's face pushed into my mind, and I forced them away. No. I wasn't interested in saving anyone. Not anymore.

I had finally completed my goal and gathered enough credit for the one thing I *did* want to buy, a weapons upgrade for my ship. Fuck yes. The Scion Spectra IV ion cannon. For several years now, I'd hunted down every Hive Soldier, Scout and Integration Unit I could find. I killed them all, without mercy, and stripped them for parts to sell to the Silver Scions. Where those Hive parts ended up or inside whom, I couldn't care less. That was not my concern. If some asshole from Rogue 5 wanted a cyborg arm or enhanced vision, good on him—as long as he paid.

"No, we do not. Stay out of my way, Isaak."

"Of course." I wasn't going to argue with her. That would be bad for business.

"Good. That's settled." Ulza stood. The elder blue female was nearly six feet tall and lined with muscle. I didn't dare take my eyes off her. The Xeriman race was known for both their bad temper and lack of control. Add the deadly fangs, and she could be truly terrifying. She was not full-blooded Xeriman. No one on Rogue 5 had pure blood left, their hybrid nature making them unpredictable.

I didn't know of her other business dealings, but I'd never once heard of her purchasing more than Hive Tech. A female? There were plenty within Cerberus legion. A human female would be... diverting, but why now? Why *this* one?

I was curious, but I did not have time for a female. A mate needed shelter. Protection. Cautious handling. I couldn't offer any of that. Not after what happened. It would be cruel and unfair to any Trion female to ask her to be mine. Cruel for me as well. It was the female who wore the chains on Trion. Marks of adornment, protection and mastery.

While it was in a Trion male's nature to control, I was

worse than most of my kind. I *needed* a female to give herself to me without inhibition. Something inside me demanded submission. Complete. Total. I would not mate unless the female gave me total trust. Consent. A mate who would allow me to care for her completely, in every way. I needed a mate who needed more from me than sex. Sex was easy. I wanted a mate who would surrender her very soul into my keeping.

The thought of taking a female against her will? Claiming her without her pleasure-filled cries? Repugnant. The idea of one being taken to Rogue 5, let alone Cerberus... she would not live long.

She must have heard me grunt in disgust. "Do you have something else to say to me?" she asked.

I shook my head, took a big swallow of my drink, wiped my mouth with the back of my hand. "Good luck."

She turned and left. No goodbyes, but we weren't friends. Our business was complete, and I had an ion cannon to pay for and finally possessed the credits to do it.

I left soon after and walked the nearly deserted corridors of Omega Dome. The scents of sweat, piss and smugglers were something I'd long ago learned to ignore. The echoing emptiness, however, was disconcerting. No one was around. There was a reason for the eerie quiet. They must be gathering inside where Jirghogis kept his merchandise to see the human.

The female Ulza intended to take to Cerberus.

I thought of my friends, Ivy and Zenos. Ivy was human, and she behaved nothing like any other female I'd ever met. She was anything but docile. In fact, I'd first assumed she was a rebel from Viken or Everis. An outcast like me. Someone who wanted to leave their past as far behind as possible. Especially once she bought the Hive tech from me and insisted I tell her how to contact the Silver Scions to have it implanted. Those implants had made Ivy stronger than most males. Her mate didn't seem to mind. Zenos of Astra legion was even bigger than an Atlan.

Thinking of Ivy and Zenos made me grin. They would be waiting for me to return to the Lelantos with my new and improved ship. They'd promised to get me drunk on the very best Atlan wine to celebrate my success before their next dangerous foray into Hive controlled space. The pair were hard core rebels who did what I did. We invaded Hive controlled space. We killed the Hive, and we sold the parts in Sector Zero.

Ivy and Zenos belonged to Astra, their leader giving them an incredible ship—the Lelantos—and free rein to fight and scavenge Hive parts. Me? I didn't belong anywhere. Trion was where I'd been raised, but I wouldn't go back there. It was my home world, but not my *home.* Not anymore.

I killed Hive. Lots and lots of them. I wasn't a Coalition fighter, but I hated the Hive and what they did to my people. To all people. Killing them was no crime, and if I managed to make a profit while I was at it? Who would judge?

I had no one out here. And this human female Jirghogis held captive for Cerberus? She would be far from home. Without hope. Friends. Protection.

The thought would not stop playing in my mind.

What would the rest of her life be like on Rogue 5 in

the most hellish of legions? Where she had no chance to escape. She'd be dead within the year... or wish to be.

"*Fark*." I cursed at no one in particular as I made my way toward the center of the domed market. I had to see this human for myself. I needed to be able to sleep at night. And besides that, if Ivy ever found out I'd left an *Earth Girl*, as she called them, to Cerberus, she would flay me alive, and Zenos would hand her the knife.

I hurried now, the roar of voices coming from the central section growing louder with each step. Those I passed ignored me, in a hurry themselves to see the rare treasure rumored to be on display. No doubt everyone under the dome knew of her presence.

"Move," I growled. I had to know.

A large space-dock worker stood, blocking my path. The male grumbled and moved aside to allow me to pass but not before glancing down at my leg where my ion blaster was strapped to my thigh.

"Good decision." Shoving past him and into the gathered crowd, I saw Ulza, her height and color making her distinct.

Pushing closer, I avoided looking up onto the platform where I knew the female stood, the response from the crowd—and the loud crack of Jirghogis' titan stick—all I needed to hear. Ulza hadn't been lying. The others from Cerberus hadn't been lying. There was a human female here who everyone wanted to lay eyes upon. Me? I did not want to look at her—not yet. Instead, I surveyed the crowd for threats. Weapons. Level of interest.

Many ogled the platform and the human female. Not

many looked as if they would dare to defy Cerberus and try to take the female.

Regardless of what this female looked like or how broken she might be, I could not allow a brute from Cerberus legion to have her. I couldn't let Ulza take her. She was my Hive Tech buyer, and she wasn't going to be pleased. *Fark*, she was going to be beyond angry. She would hunt me down for crossing her.

Gods be damned. I was cursed. *Fark*. Cursed with a conscience I did not want. I should go buy my *farking* Spectra IV ion cannon and get out of the sector at high speed. But no. Apparently, I had not learned my lesson. But this time, it wouldn't be my brother dying, it would me.

Like it should have been five years ago.

I risked looking up onto the platform, flicked my gaze past Jirghogis, and my heart stopped.

Rich brown hair kissed with streaks of gold hung past her shoulders. She wore plain brown pants and tunic, covering her skin from my sight, but the curves beneath the snug fabric were lush and full, and I ached to trace every contour. She wore a golden collar around her neck, the site making my cock tighten with the unwelcome thought that she should be wearing *my* collar around her neck. It should be my golden chain disappearing beneath her clothing. I would adorn her properly and dress her in the softest silks were she mine.

Which she was not and never would be. She was a prisoner waiting for transfer, if the manacle around her ankle was any indication. But it was her gaze that held me captive.

Blue-green eyes stared defiantly out over the crowd.

She studied the room, her stare lingering on those I considered to be the most dangerous. I wondered how she knew, where she had learned to recognize and evaluate the most deadly criminals in the room?

She was a beauty beyond compare. The fire in her eyes forced a reluctant admiration to stir deep within me —where before there had been nothing but ash and sorrow, something new pulsed to life.

Hunger. Curiosity. A fierce need to protect.

Ulza moved forward, closer to the stage, and the female I was determined to save looked down her nose at her like a queen dismissing a rodent.

The blue barbarian growled. Ulza was here to deliver the human to Cerberus.

I discreetly did a weapons check. Ion blaster. Dagger. Second dagger. Poison powder. The urge to kill.

I had them all. No one was going to touch that female unless it was me.

And if she refused me?

Well, I would escort her back to her home planet...and do my damndest to seduce her every step of the way.

3

ara, Sector Zero, Planet Occeron, Omega Dome

I LOOKED out over the crowd that gathered at my feet, stared beyond the stage I'd been chained to like a pagan offering to the gods, and saw nothing familiar. Nothing clean. Nothing that gave me the slightest bit of hope.

I'd thought the desert tent planet was different, but this? This was where... *Mad Max* met the shady cantina in *Star Wars.* I felt like Princess Leia before Jabba the Hut, but instead of the gold bikini, I wore an ugly brown pair of pants and tunic that covered me from shoulders to knees. It effectively hid the line of the chain that dangled between my breasts, and the darker rose of my nipples. I was naked beneath. I'd never been modest, but I was grateful to be covered. It would appear that Bertok wasn't selling me for sex.

Actually, it would appear that I wasn't being sold at all.

A delivery, Bertok had said, handing me off to Jirghogis in trade for what I assumed was space money. What the hell I was supposed to deliver and to whom, I had no idea. But I didn't like the looks of this place.

I knew no one here. Hell, anyone I knew was on Earth, light years away. Besides, I was human. What everyone else in the place was, I had no idea. Some were even fucking blue, and I didn't mean they were holding their breath. Some had horns. Some had faces covered with a strange rough fur that looked almost like porcupine needles. Others looked like walking reptiles—their eyes orange or yellow, and their pupils slit like a snake's. When the nearest whipped a forked tongue in my direction, I choked down a scream and looked away. I would not give the slime-coated monster who had nudged me out here with the end of his pseudo-cattle prod the satisfaction of screaming.

But no. Just no. This was not okay.

I had no idea what planet Bertok had transported me to. Why he'd sold me to the creepy guy with slimy scales and the hideous tail or where Bertok was now. I didn't have a clue why I was here. How I'd get off the planet. I didn't have a weapon. Hell, I didn't even have shoes.

But the desire burning in my gut was pure fire.

Bertok.

I was going to survive this, and I was going to hunt the fucker down and string his guts across the desert sands of Trion for vultures—did Trion have vultures?—to tear apart. He'd killed my mate. For that alone, he deserved to die. I was not a soft, shy, innocent woman. Bertok made a mistake taking me. I'd grown up poor, on the streets, scrapping with the gangs and the pimps and the drug dealers. I knew how to survive, how to fight, how to take care of my damn self.

This place was no different. Wherever here was. I'd hoped that the Interstellar Brides Program would be different. I had actually believed I could escape my life. The system.

Wrong, Zara. Way fucking wrong.

I had no idea how I was going to get out of here, out of this mess, but I hadn't survived the streets and the rough life that went with it to just give in now and be a slave.

No fucking way.

This place, with rowdy, drunken patrons, was a shithole full of alien criminals. It took one to know one, even in space. Scum was scum, no matter what kind of skin, fur or scales they were covered with.

I laughed to myself. If these assholes only knew. I might be female, and I might be from Earth, and I might be tiny, but I was fucking fierce. I wasn't to be handled carefully because I was a dainty flower. No, I had to be handled carefully because I was an atomic bomb.

Justice. I'd get justice for Naron. For myself.

I'd track Bertok down, slit his throat like he had Naron's and then make my way home. It wouldn't be the first time I had survived, despite the odds stacked against me. I'd handled and even tamed the streets when I was a teen. I would survive. Not just survive. Bertok was going to pay. For killing my mate in cold blood. For crushing the one and only dream I'd allowed myself since I was too young to remember dreaming about a different life.

"It's time for you to go. Cerberus is here." The

creature holding the electric stick struck it along the hard, cold floor just a few inches in front of my feet, and I jerked back instinctively, trying to distance myself from the threat. When I looked back at him, his lecherous gaze was on my chest, a thick, heavy drool the likes of which I'd never seen from anything resembling a man, dripped from his scaly lips like he was drooling over a bone. So gross. His spit smelled rotten, like burned hair and sulfur.

I didn't know what he was talking about or what Cerberus was.

When he poked at the ground again, I did not move. His grin turned to a scowl, but I looked away. I would not perform for him. Not fight or wiggle and shake my breasts for his amusement. Would. Not. The clothes were brown and heavy enough to keep me warm, but they were tight. Too damn tight. And though small, I was not a flat-chested woman.

The slimy auctioneer bent down and pushed a series of buttons on the stage. At once, the manacle around my ankle dropped to the floor, deactivated by whatever magic button he had just pushed.

I didn't know who my escort was in this crowd, but I wasn't waiting to find out. Not now that I was no longer shackled.

This was it. It was go/no-go time. If I escaped now, I'd remain free or die. If I let some escort take me, I was as good as dead. There was no choice. Now was it. I took a deep breath, let it out.

The scaly creature made the pokey stick sizzle again, but this time, I stepped back and grabbed it in the center, as far from the activated tip as I could get. Clearly, he wasn't expecting me to fight back. Tugging hard, it ripped from his so-called fingers, and I spun it around like a fucking cheerleader's baton then lunged. The crackle of the stick this time was against his flesh.

He bellowed in agony as I held it in place, probably not in the way the tool was supposed to be used. What-fucking-ever.

I shoved once more, then pulled back. He slumped forward in blatant pain. Good.

With a running leap, I jumped off the raised platform and into the crowd. They were smarter than the scaly one, for they made a path for me. Or, they made a path for the electric cattle prod.

I waved it in front of me, kept the path going. I'd seen people... beings, coming in and out from the far corner, so that was where I was headed. A corridor. A hallway. Somewhere, this place had to have a transport room. And if not? Well, there had to be ships out here. I'd steal one. Kidnap a pilot. Whatever I had to do.

"Stop the human!"

A blue female got in my way. Her? *She* was my escort? She stood in my path, eyes narrowed, clearly not afraid of me and eager to halt my retreat. "You Cerberus?"

"You will come with me." She spoke clearly, slowly, making sure my translator thing had time to process her order.

"No." I lifted the stick higher, waved it in front of her. She didn't budge. I lunged like a samurai and got her in the torso. Not even a flicker of pain. Did she have zero pain receptors or was she wearing something that blocked the charge? Either way, the stick only made her smile. "You belong to Cerberus, female. You will not run from me."

Fuck. I tried again. Her eyes narrowed, and she took a step toward me. I widened my stance, ready for a catfight. I hated fighting other women. They were ruthless. But I was not going with her. Not happening.

One second, she was ready to take me out, the next she was shoved out of the way as if she were a forward who'd been body-checked at the World Cup. A guy, who looked more human than the blue female stood before me with a pretty serious scowl on his face. He'd tackled the blue alien, but when he straightened to his full— gorgeous—height, he didn't look happy about it.

"Thanks," I murmured, not sure he would welcome the sentiment.

"I'm an idiot." He ducked a punch to the head coming from his left. I whipped the electrical stick around like a baton and zapped the offender, who screeched like an injured owl and whirled away. I gripped the stick and whipped it around, keeping everyone else as far from us as possible.

"Thanks," he offered right back, the corner of his mouth tipped up.

"Stop them!" Jirghogis shouted. I recognized his slithery voice.

The guy narrowed his eyes and hardened his jaw as he grabbed my wrist. "Time to go, *gara*."

Tall, dark and handsome tugged me toward the exit. I didn't know if he was a good guy or a bad guy, but he was helping me get out of here.

I'd decide later if I should zap him or not.

He was strong and had his shit dialed in because he kept a hold of my wrist and cleared a path for us as if chopping through a jungle with a machete. He didn't stop when we were outside the place but tugged me along behind him. I had to run to keep up with his long-legged gait.

Glancing up, it appeared as if we were inside some kind of snow globe. There was no breeze or change in temperature. We weren't *outside.*

I followed for a few minutes as he took various paths between buildings just as I would have on Earth to avoid being followed. Only when we ducked into an alley of some sort did he stop.

He looked me over, breathing hard. While he did that, I scoped him out in return, holding my weapon at the ready. He appeared to be helping me, but I wasn't taking any chances. And the fact that he was moderately attractive was *not* going to influence my decision.

Nope. Not at all. He was *not* sexy. He was an alien. I needed to remember that.

"Thanks for saving me back there," I said.

"You were doing a pretty good job all on your own. You're skilled with a titan stick. Got those on Earth?"

I laughed. "No, but I'm skilled at dealing with assholes. They usually aren't blue though."

This guy, he wasn't blue. He looked... not blue. I couldn't say *normal* because I had a feeling I was the *not* normal one around here. But he looked more human than anyone else as I'd seen.

Dark hair in need of a haircut. I had a feeling it was long enough to go into a tie, but he kept it down. Piercing dark eyes. Scruff on his square jaw. He was big, well over six feet, but not huge like an Atlan I'd seen on the Bachelor Beast show on TV. He wore all black, and a weapon was strapped to his thigh.

I had to admit, he was really attractive. Hot. Ruggedly handsome. I felt small beside him, but unlike the milling group of thugs, or even Bertok, I didn't feel threatened. His gaze held heat but more frustration and some anger although I didn't think it was directed at me.

He was calm, which meant this kind of action wasn't new for him.

I looked into his eyes again, and they were focused squarely on mine.

"You'll want to steer clear of the Ulza." He thumbed over his shoulder.

"The blue lady?"

"Yes, she's part of Cerberus legion. She's also a Xeriman hybrid, which makes her meaner than most."

"I don't know what any of that is but noted." No sense lying.

"Red arm bands. All different hybrid species. They're everywhere in the dome."

"Ah, gang colors?" I knew all about that. And looking back, both the hard-as-nails blue woman and a bunch of creepers in the ogle-fest had been wearing dark red bands around their biceps, bands the color of red wine. Or blood.

"Where is Cerberus?" I'd never heard of that planet before, but I'd make a mental note not to go there.

"It's not a place, it's a—never mind. Just steer clear of them."

"I'd like to steer clear of this entire planet," I added. There didn't seem to be one redeeming thing about the place. It was dirty. It smelled. And the inhabitants were barbarians.

"*Fark.*" He ran his hand through his hair and looked

down the alley. His square jaw line was prominent with his head turned. Why was I attracted to a guy now? Here? I was in danger. I didn't have a clue where I was. I didn't even have shoes. Yet I wanted to feel if his hair was silky soft. If he was as muscular as he appeared. If he would feel strong and powerful beneath my palms. If he would take me like the alien I'd been with in my processing dream, dominant, bossy, and very, very dedicated to giving me pleasure.

My pulse rocketed up a notch, and my breasts ached, heavy with need. What. The. Hell?

Shit. I was going crazy.

"I can't believe I helped you," he muttered.

My mouth fell open. He actually was pissed, but it wasn't my fault. "I didn't ask for your help. I was doing fine on my own," I snapped. "Like you said, I can use this thing." I waved the cattle prod in the air.

My *rescuer* took a half step closer, so I had to tilt my chin up. "Yeah, I saw that. The blue female, she was supposed to deliver you to Cerberus legion on Rogue 5."

I had no idea where that was either, and I didn't care to find out. "Not happening. The way you took her out, it doesn't seem like you two are friends."

He frowned. "Friends? Never. Now? We're enemies." He looked at his wrist, at some kind of small screen. "*Fark.* She retracted her credit. And she has the integrations." He paced in a circle with his hands on his hips.

"What does that even mean?" I wondered.

"I sold her something. Earlier. After our little... escape, she retracted her credit."

"Space money."

"Yes," he confirmed. "She wasn't happy I got in her way."

I bit my lip. "Sorry." I wasn't, but it probably wouldn't be smart to say so right now.

He set his hands on his hips and paced, lost in his angry thoughts.

I took a step back while he was distracted then another. He might be broody and gorgeous, but he also ran hot, which meant he was unpredictable. I was better off looking at him in my rearview mirror.

He looked up, took in the distance between us. "Where are you going?"

I thumbed over my shoulder like he had. "Trion."

His dark gaze lowered to my breasts then widened. How he hadn't noticed the outline of the chain through my tight brown tunic, I had no idea, but the swaying golden links and the piercings they were attached to were clear as day now that my nipples were hard as rocks. Damn it.

"Trion. Why do you want to go there?"

"I was brought here from Trion and given to the stinky lizard guy. Well, not given. Actually, I was unconscious for most of it, so I don't know how I got here. But I do know who to blame. I'm going to make Bertok regret it."

"Bertok?" The guy's mouth fell open.

"You know him?"

"He's a Councilor on Trion. *He* sold you to Jirghogis?"

I didn't really know what a Councilor was, but it was something important on Trion. I nodded. "He's also a douche canoe who killed my mate, so he could sell me here on... wherever the fuck we are."

31

When his eyes widened in surprise, I couldn't miss how dark they were. He stepped close and cupped my jaw. "You had a Trion mate?"

"For all of two minutes," I grumbled then moved away from his touch. He was surprisingly gentle for a guy who had such rough edges.

I thought of Naron. He hadn't had any rough edges, at least from what I'd been able to tell. I didn't mourn him because I knew him. I mourned him because he'd been an innocent caught up in Bertok's fucked up plans. And because he represented a dream, a dream that had died with him.

My rescuer stepped toward me, all swagger and dark brooding. "Are you telling me you're an Interstellar Bride?"

I shrugged again. "Not any longer. My mate's dead. I'm going back to Earth."

He laughed *at* me, and that totally pissed me off.

"*Gara*, you're a citizen of Trion now. Not Earth."

That word, that endearment, was what Naron had called me, too. The word from this male's lips affected me like he'd licked my skin, the sound sensual and threatening all at once. And that double-edged sword made me want him close. Made me want to trust him. Which was stupid. Just fucking stupid.

"Don't call me that." I moved to stand toe to boot with him, but I had to tip my chin back even further to meet his eyes.

"Then tell me your name, human," he countered.

"Zara."

He said it aloud, as if testing the sound of it on his

32

tongue. "There isn't much difference between Zara and *gara*, now is there?"

I rolled my eyes.

He smirked.

"Well?" I waited.

He frowned. "Well, what?"

"Your name."

"Isaak."

"Isaak, I will go home to Earth. It hasn't been thirty days yet," I countered.

Slowly, he shook his head. "Trion's in a different part of the galaxy. When you transport to and from Trion, time bends."

"Bends? What does that mean?" I crossed my arms over my chest, felt the chain press into the backs of my arms.

"It means when you are on Trion, three months pass out here in a blink."

My mouth fell open. "Three months? That wasn't on *Star Trek* or *Battlestar Galactica.*"

He frowned. "I don't know what that means, but Earth's out for you. You're never going back. You are a citizen of Trion, and since you're past your thirty days and your mate is dead, you are a widow. You will not be assigned another mate by the program."

"I've been in space all of a day, as far as I can tell."

He studied me, and when his fingers lifted to my jaw again, I had to clench my teeth to keep from leaning into the touch. It was as if my body was starving for any amount of comfort it could get. Not that I could blame myself. The last day and a half had been hell on a whole new level.

"How many hours were you on Trion? Before you transported here?"

I wasn't sure, but Bertok said he had to wait to transport me again, so I wouldn't get sick or die. So who knew? "Overnight maybe. A day? Maybe a bit longer. I don't know for sure. I slept part of it."

Isaak's dark eyes filled with pity, and the sight made me angry all over again. Completely ruined the soft, warm touch of his fingertips on my jaw. And the thought that I mourned the loss at all made me twice as angry even before he opened his mouth.

"*Gara,* every hour on Trion is more than a day and a half out here."

I paused because his words rang with finality. They were also what Warden Egara had said—the part of being a citizen of Trion—right before she'd had a machine jab an NPU behind my ear. As for being a widow, that wasn't mentioned. The death of a mate within five minutes of transport by throat slice was probably a little depressing to tell bride volunteers. "Fine, I can't go back to Earth. So what? I'm still going to Trion. I've got a score to settle."

He looked me over again, and this time, I wanted to punch the smirk off his face. "You're a tiny thing but ruthless." He leaned in close, almost as if he couldn't help himself. "I like that."

"Yeah, don't forget it." I held his gaze, but I was having trouble getting enough air into my lungs. Why was he still *touching me?* Totally distracting. I shoved his hand away. "Don't do that again. Don't touch me."

He frowned. "You're not my prisoner. I *helped* you to escape. I'm not like them."

I had managed to offend him at last. "We'll see."

"I would never force myself on a female. Never."

His hands clenched into fists at his sides, and his eyes darkened to the point where I could no longer see the center. His skin flushed, and his pulse raced at the base of his neck. He was beyond angry.

"Good to know." I meant it, but I wasn't going to apologize for protecting myself. Nor was I going to give him a gold star because he believed in consent.

I believed him. He didn't have to help me escape to harm me. He could have beaten me, raped me or knocked me out cold by now, if that's what he wanted. But I had learned to read people, and everything about this guy—except the fact that he was an alien—told me I could trust him. At least for now.

"What?" he asked as I stared at him.

I waggled my finger toward his face. "All that handsomeness would be wasted if you were an asshole."

A slow smile grew. "You think I'm handsome?"

"Well, you aren't covered in scales or poison slime."

He stiffened as if offended. "You have very low standards for a male."

I grinned and enjoyed teasing him. I didn't have the time or inclination to stroke his ego. He was hot. Like, rip his clothes off hot. But I didn't know him. I didn't know where I was. My mate was dead. I couldn't go home. I had nothing. No one. Nada. So I focused on the one thing I did know. The one thing out here that made sense to me.

"If you know Bertok, then you're from Trion." I didn't state it as a question. When he'd noticed the piercings on my breasts, he'd recognized them for what they were: a Trion adornment.

His eyes widened again as if I continued to surprise him. "Yes."

"Great. Then you can take me back. Do you have a ship?" I looked around as if it were a car parked on a street.

His gaze narrowed.

That was a yes if I ever saw one. "So, you do have a ship. The big blue lady's going to track you down to get even, so why not head to Trion right now?"

"I will never return to Trion." He turned on his heel and walked at a pace that forced me to run to keep up, as if he were walking away from more than me. "I will take you to Ivy and Zenos. Then you will be their problem."

I wasn't quite sure who Ivy and Zenos were, but I jogged and stared at his ass as I did so, glad for the time I'd spent exercising on Earth. Being able to run had meant survival for me on more than one occasion. "What about the scaly alien? The one covered in slime?"

"Jirghogis? He is not my problem. Based on what you said, you've got bigger ones. Like Bertok and Cerberus." He ran a hand over his face then started walking again. "*Fark*, human. When you get in a mess, you don't go small," he said as he went.

I let him walk off. He might be good on the eyes, but he was a pain in the ass. And he'd refused to take me where I wanted to go. For all I knew, this Ivy and Zenos were blue and slimy, respectively. No, thank you.

I turned back the way we had come. There had been several smaller corridors along the way. I would find somewhere to hide. Steal some clothing and food. Look around, find a transport room or two and get the hell off this planet. If this Cerberus guy wanted me, if some blue lady was around probably trying to find me, I had to be gone. Pronto.

I'd transport to Trion and hunt down Bertok. Kill him.

Then I'd go home. I didn't care what the law was. The Coalition and their Brides Program could go to hell. I was not staying out here. I was going to make sure Bertok could never hurt anyone else, ever again, and then I was going home.

Life sucked everywhere. At least on Earth, I knew the rules and how to break them without getting killed.

4

saak

"*FARK*. STUBBORN FEMALE," I muttered.

Tangling with the human had done irreparable damage to my equilibrium. I had not been this frustrated since I'd left Trion behind.

Her eyes spit fire, and all I wanted to do was accept the challenge, push her up against the wall, drive my cock deep and make her scream with pleasure. Which was completely opposite of every Trion female. Ever. I wanted a docile female. Meek. Submissive. Yet the Gods had set this wild Earthling in my path.

Nothing she had done was as expected. She did not tremble with fear after nearly being taken by a huge blue alien from Cerberus legion. She did not cry. She had stolen Jirghogis' titan stick and threatened him with it like a cornered animal.

Like a wild animal.

Untamed.

I wondered what it would take to tame her in my bed.

My cock swelled to uncomfortable weight, and I cursed again. No. I would not become involved in this drama. I had offered her escape, a meeting with Ivy, a female from her own planet. I had wrecked my business alliance as well as cost myself a *farking* fortune already. I was *not* going to follow that female. I was *not* going to protect her from her own stubborn, reckless courage. She was not mine.

"Not mine." I would have chanted the words to myself if I'd been able to get the vision of her eyes lit from within by cold rage. By challenge. She had not trembled, even when I'd touched her, when the lure of her soft skin had become too powerful to resist. No, she'd stood her ground and verbally sparred with me. She was like a charged ion blast waiting to go off.

Everything she said was a surprise. I hadn't known what to expect out of such a tiny human, but...sass wasn't one of them. Spunk. Fire. Passion.

My ship wasn't far. I could be off this rock—without my ion cannon—in no time at all and leave her to her dangerous and insane plans for revenge.

"*Fark.*" My feet stopped moving of their own volition. Gods be damned. I couldn't *farking* do it. I couldn't walk away. Seemed I had some small shred of decency left. And it would, no doubt, damn me to a painful end. Over a female who wasn't even mine.

Perhaps it was cosmic justice. So be it.

Expecting to see her behind me, I looked back and... she'd walked *away from me*. She was leaving me intentionally to make her own way with only a titan stick for protection. And she was nearly out of sight.

Damn stubborn female. She did not know what she was dealing with here. This was Sector Zero, for *fark's* sake! No female was left unattended. She was too valuable, too precious... too beautiful. Anyone would want her. Claim her. Own her. Whether she consented or not.

Hadn't she learned that? If some alien found her, he'd keep her. It was as simple and lawless as that.

It wasn't my job to protect her. Besides, she didn't want my protection. Zara was free. She was choosing to go after Bertok. Alone. She was an Interstellar Bride. If the Coalition had any fighters in this sector, they would protect her, without question.

But we weren't in Coalition space. Hell, there hadn't been a Coalition fighter in this sector for over a hundred years. Odds were not good that one had taken a wrong turn back to his battlegroup. That he would make his way here and arrive just in time to save the beautiful female from a terrible fate.

"*Fark.*"

The lawless factions here were probably already searching for her. She was perfect. Soft, creamy skin. The long, curled hair. The defiance in her eyes. She could have passed for a Trionite, if pushed, especially with the gold collar and the outline of the chain I'd seen dangling between her nipples. *Fark* if that didn't make me hard. But no, there was too much defiance in her gaze for Trion to have been her home. The women of Viken and my home world of Trion were submissive and soft. Fragile creatures that needed to be both pampered and protected. They loved to show off their bond, proud to have their mate's medallion dangling upon a chain. Everyone could look upon her beauty—even in the throes of passion. Our females often enjoyed knowing they were coveted by others but could not be touched by any but their mate.

"Damn it, female," I called, letting my head fall back, I stared up at the dome. "Stop. Do you want to be a slave? Tortured? Raped? Used?"

She turned on her heel to face me and placed her hands on her hips in a defiant gesture that made my cock harden with lust and my dominant nature rise to accept her challenge.

Perhaps this was why I had yet to be interested in mating a female. All the females I had met on Trion were meek, raised to be submissive, in bed and out. Mild. Tame.

This human was the opposite. How the *fark* had she been matched to Trion? It made no sense because here was a female worthy of being tamed. Claimed. Her submission would be hard won and worth the effort.

"You don't even know where you are."

"Enlighten me then," she countered.

I took a deep breath, let it out and closed the distance between us. "Sector Zero. This outpost survives on a large planet called Occeron. It used to be full of life. But now, there's no atmosphere. Battle with the Hive destroyed the planet's magnetic field. The only thing that survives does so underground or sealed inside protective domes like the one above our heads."

Her eyes lifted skyward. At least she was listening.

"This place is called Omega Dome. It was designed to hold three thousand inhabitants. This one shields five times that. While some might *live* here, all they do is survive."

"Why are you here then?"

"Business."

"Yeah, well, it's my business to transport out of this snow globe and hunt down Bertok."

"And how are you going to do that?" I didn't ask what a snow globe was. I understood her intent.

"I'll ask the slimy one." She tapped the titan stick on the ground for emphasis, indicating exactly who she intended to make him talk.

Ah. So, she did intend to go after Jirghogis as well as the Trion Councilor. "That slime is poisonous," I warned.

Her mouth fell open. "Then I'll interrogate him without touching him, which I preferred to do anyway. He smells like a dead horse." She shivered in what I guessed was revulsion as I had no idea what a horse was. I didn't blame her. Jirghoghis was repulsive. "After that, I'm going to go to Trion and kill Bertok. Then I'm going home."

Yes, my cock hardened at her daring plan. It was the intent behind it that made my balls ache. The surety of it. It was as if these kinds of obstacles were not hard for her. As if she'd survived similar dark challenges on her home planet.

"No, you will do none of those things. They are too dangerous." I stepped even closer, moving at a steady speed, not wanting to scare her.

"I don't belong to you." The female stood barefoot yet

defiant. The rings in her nipples only had a plain chain strung between them... I was sure of it. No medallion hung pressed to the fabric covering her, none that I could see. I hoped suddenly that she was unadorned. Unclaimed.

She claimed her mate was dead, but what if she were mistaken? What if there was a male back on Trion looking for her?

I looked closely, uncaring if she noticed my interest. There was nothing that indicated a family medallion had been included in her adornments. *Fark*, I could even see the outline of a chain, the rings on her nipples. But no family medallion. No proper adornments. Nothing that would protect her. No claim by a mate.

Strangely, I could see the outline of something piercing her navel as well. This was not Trion custom.

So why did she have it? From what I knew of human females from Ivy, piercing was not a normal custom on Earth, and I doubted a pierced navel offered any kind of sexual satisfaction.

Perhaps she liked to be adorned. Liked the glide of metal over her soft skin. Perhaps, she would also enjoy metal binding her wrists and ankles as I filled her from behind.

The thought burst across my mind like a comet, and my casual inspection turned to lust. Perhaps she was matched to Trion because she needed to submit, to surrender to her lover. Perhaps her outspoken and independent side longed for an outlet, a place to feel safe, cared for. Protected. Perhaps, underneath the bluster lived a female with a truly submissive nature. Perhaps she wasn't even aware of what she needed.

Not perhaps. She *wasn't* aware. I'd bet my Spectra IV on that.

The realization made me smile. *Fark.* She would welcome my dominant nature. My need to control her pleasure. She would surrender control.

To me.

She held my gaze far longer than I thought possible for a fragile female, even when I placed my hand over my ion blaster to test her resolve. That move did inspire movement but not what I had in mind.

"Spare me the drama." She waved a hand in the air. "If you were an asshole, you would have shot me already. I know a thug when I see one." She turned away from me again. *Dismissed* me.

"You will not return to the market to search for Jirghogis," I ordered. "They'll capture you, and you will never be free of their shackles. You've shamed him and Ulza."

"Bye!" She yelled the single word and waved the titan stick up over her head, the crackling sound loud in the enclosed space as she activated the weapon once more, tapping the electrified end on the bracing bars that held up the ceiling in this section of the dome. A loud buzz and crackle were accompanied by a shower of sparks that fell behind her like small fires before they hit the floor and died out.

I stood, undecided, as she disappeared around a corner.

I *should* allow her to go. She'd made her choice. I had done what I had to in order to save her. My conscience was clear.

"*Fark.*" That was a lie. She was going to get herself

killed. I couldn't allow that, and I had to know what it would be like to feel all that energy, all that angst, come from her in passion instead of rage. I could be that outlet for her. The conduit to her ultimate release.

If I could get us both out of Omega Dome alive.

5

Zara

I HAD no idea where I was going. I thought I was headed back toward the place where the slimy guy'd held me... waiting for what, I had no idea. But now I was lost. This was like an inner- city slum with no escape. There was literally a bubble over the place—the only way out, I assumed, was either by transport or a spaceship. I knew more than I wanted about transport, like the fact that it hurt like being blasted all over with ice, that transporting from Earth to Trion had worn me out, and that I had absolutely no idea how to operate one of the transport things, even if I could find one. That was one too many obstacles, even for me.

That blue lady was probably pissed I'd gotten away and was searching for me. Transport would be the last place I'd go. I knew nothing about space ships except what I saw on TV. It wasn't like I could steal one and fly out of here. If I could find the ignition, I'd probably crash before I got twenty feet off the ground. And if I miraculously made it out of the bubble... I assumed there was some kind of hatch or something... I had no idea where I was going. Did they take gas? Were there refill stations in space?

Maybe I could find a nice space pirate and pay him— or her—to get me out of here.

But with what? I didn't have space money. And I wasn't interested in selling myself. I'd managed to avoid that life growing up surrounded by addicts so desperate they would sell their soul for a hit. But I wasn't that desperate. At least not yet.

Fuck. Fuck. Fuck. I was so screwed.

I stopped, groaned, tugged on my hair. Maybe the hottie was right. If I went after slimy guy, I'd be walking right back into something I'd fought my way out of. Yes, I was mad, hurt, lost. But I wasn't stupid. And I would be an idiot to go back to slime-tail looking for a fight. It was important to know when to retreat and live to fight another day.

A hand gripped my arm, and I jumped a foot, then instinct kicked in. I dropped my shoulders, leaned forward and bent my elbow up and back. Hard.

"*Fark!*" The hold disappeared, and I tried to run, my heart rate going faster than my feet. "Zara, wait."

I stopped, practically skidding to a halt. Turning on my heel, there was Isaak holding his nose. Exhaling, I tried to let the adrenaline bleed out. "Don't grab me like that," I snapped, walking back to him. "You're lucky I didn't go for your balls instead."

He dropped his hands and frowned. "Where did you learn to defend yourself like that?"

I crossed my arms over my chest. "Earth."

His frown only grew. "Why does a female need to know such things?"

Narrowing my gaze, I glared. I wasn't going to tell him that protecting myself had become second nature. "You snuck up on me to ask me questions about Earth?"

He sighed. "You can't get away from Sector Zero without a ship. Transport is—"

"Not an option," I finished.

Nodding, he continued. "Ulza knows me. She knows I helped you. The first place she's going to go is the transport pad. The second is the landing bay. I'm headed there now to get away from Sector Zero. You have five seconds to decide if you are coming with me or staying here."

There wasn't much choice. In fact, there was *no* choice.

"You'll take me with you? But where are you going?"

"Three, two—"

"I'm going with you." I didn't care much where we went. I'd take my chances with Isaak one-on-one. Even if he turned out to be a bad guy, I'd rather deal with just one than an entire dome full of criminals hunting me.

He nodded, then took my hand and started running. I had to sprint to keep up with his long legs, careful to keep the titan stick up and away from my feet. I kept it turned on. Well, I had no idea how to turn it off. It wasn't like a toy light saber with a button that I could find. Every once in a while, it would hit the wall and sparks would fly.

"Stop doing that," he snapped over his shoulder. "You'll draw too much attention."

I looked around. We were sprinting through corridors lined with people. Some held more than others, but still. "We're running. People are already looking at us."

"People run. Nothing new. But there's only one titan stick on this rock, and everyone knows exactly who it belongs to. And it's not you." He was barely breathing hard, and I had to admire his stamina. My adrenaline rush was on the downward spiral, and I was running on fumes.

"Shit." So, I'd stolen slimy-tail's famous weapon? And it was one of a kind?

I couldn't help the grin, the smile growing to a full-blown cheek buster the more I thought about it. Good. I hoped the thing cost a fortune. But I did make sure not to strike any more walls.

We ran for what felt like forever but was probably only a few minutes. I was gasping by the time we reached what looked like a huge ship holding area. There was one gigantic exit that seemed to be closed in with a forcefield of some kind. Very SciFi Channel. Beyond that, I saw nothing but blackness. And stars. No blue sky and mountains. No trees. Nothing but barren rocks and... space.

I froze in awe. I was really and truly in outer space. Like, walk on the moon, go to Mars, go to Trion, outer freaking space. "Holy shit."

"*Fark*." Isaak pulled me to one side, hard enough that I stumbled into him.

"Hey! What—"

He cut me off with a kiss. Um, what? His mouth was on mine.

On. Mine.

Holy hell, did he know how to kiss! After the day I'd had, I sank into it, let myself enjoy the heat of him pressed to my body, the feel of his hand burning into my hip. The other cradled the back of my head like I was treasured. His heat seeped into me, and I realized this place was cold. Scary and horrible and cold. And I very much needed to be warm.

Long moments passed, and I kissed him back, not even taking time to wonder *why* he was kissing me here, now. I rolled the taste of him around on my tongue. His flavor was like exotic whiskey and man. I wondered what he'd been drinking to make him so... delicious or if it was just *him*.

I melted. My mind screamed at me that this was insane, but my body and my soul had taken enough for the day. Both needed one good moment to rest. To heal. To not be scared out of our collective fucking mind because within two minutes of transporting off of Earth, life had been one hell after another.

"*Gara.*" Isaak tore his mouth from mine, and I would have slumped into the wall next to me if not for his hands still wrapped around me. "*Fark.*" His dark eyes roved over my face, rested on my lips as if he wanted to go back for seconds. And thirds. "I should not have done that."

I blinked. Tried to think. Found the task to be extremely difficult while drowning in his stare. I licked my lips, trying to get more of his taste. "Why did you?"

"We are being hunted." He used his gaze to motion over my shoulder, and I turned my head as far as his grip in my hair would allow to see two frighteningly massive aliens wearing red arm bands, waving weapons around and yelling at a small group of people. "They are looking for a couple fleeing, not kissing."

I blinked, tried to clear my muzzy head. "These are the people who work for Cerberus," I said, trying to understand.

He nodded. "Cerberus is the leader of the Cerberus legion on Rogue 5. To you, it means nothing. To the rest of the galaxy, it means trouble. Big trouble. The red arm band signifies their allegiance to him, to the legion and to all they stand for, none of it good."

The fantasy bubble burst, and my brain took control in one second flat. "Where is your ship?" I didn't pull away from him because I didn't want to move enough to draw attention. We were in trouble here. The kiss might have delayed the bad guys seeing us while doing a quick scan of the busy landing bay, but we wouldn't be able to hide forever. And there were probably more of the bad guys from this... Cerberus legion coming.

Using my hair, he gently turned my face toward him. "Behind me. Three docks down on the left."

Without moving my head, I peeked around the corner wall, where we'd been hiding in a kind of nook lined with beams, to see spaceship-sized parking spaces painted on the floor in bright, reflective orange. Each space had a strange set of symbols on them. The ship he'd indicated was smaller than the rest. Much smaller. "The little one?"

His spine stiffened, and his chest rose, rubbing against my all-too sensitive nipples. I drew in a sharp breath as he answered me. "My ship is built for stealth."

His voice was low and practically snarled. Yeah, even guys in space had size issues.

"Okay. But can it make the Kessel Run in less than twelve parsecs?" I couldn't help myself. I was feeling the *Star Wars,* Princess Lea vibe and had to quote her.

His brows drew down. "What is a Kessel Run? It is not in any sector I know of."

I shook my head, realizing watching science fiction and *living* it were two different things entirely. "Nevermind." Stealth sounded good to me. "How do we get over there without getting killed? Or worse... captured?"

His mouth opened in surprise at my questions but continued to look down at me, and his gaze lingered on my still wet lips. "We run."

"What if someone tries to stop us?" I looked around his shoulder again. Leaned farther out to get a better look at the rest of the landing bay. There were probably half a dozen aliens of various sorts standing between us and his ship. None of them had red arm bands, but that didn't mean much as far as I was concerned.

"We shoot them."

Shoot them. God.

All I'd wanted to do was settle in with a nice mate. Nothing more. Shooting people was a main reason I'd left Earth. I was right back where I started from except now, I was in a place I didn't know, with customs and rules that were over my head. This was *worse* than home.

No, Boston wasn't *home* any longer. I could never go back. I wanted to cry. This was just too much for one fucking day. I was used to dealing with a lot of shit at one time, but I was approaching overload. I licked my lips again. "I don't have a gun."

He grinned and tapped his thigh, which I had to admit looked mighty sexy with a holster strapped to it and a weapon that might just save us. "I get the ion pistol. Time for you to use that titan stick, *gara.*"

"It's Zara," I corrected. "Zara with a Z."

His answer was the way the corner of his mouth tipped up before giving me a quick kiss on the lips. I didn't have the heart to protest. "Ready?"

I took a deep breath and checked in with myself. Was I ready? No. Not really. My heart was pounding, my palms were sweaty, my nipples were still hard from his kiss, and despite every ounce of good sense, I was putting my life in the hands of a complete stranger that I'd known all of ten or fifteen minutes. Oh, *and* I might have to fight my way out of here with a cattle prod while he killed alien bad guys.

But if *he* got killed, I was done for. I had no clue how to fly, and I'd be stuck in this crappy place until I was caught. It would only be a matter of time. "Yes. I'm ready."

I sooo wasn't ready.

He nodded, pushed me gently away from him, so he could pull the space gun from the holster. Yeah, still sexy.

Before we moved, I had to know. I gripped his arm. "Who are you, Isaak? What are *you* doing here in this place if you hate it so much? Are you a space pirate or what?"

He pressed a finger to my lips. "Later, *gara.* First, we escape. *Then* we talk."

I pursed my lips, not thrilled with the answer, and I realized I was stalling. "Fine." Noise was building behind me, and I had a sneaking suspicion the Cerberus guys were getting closer.

His eyes narrowed as he said, "We go in three. Three. Two. Go!"

He darted from our pseudo hiding space pulling me behind him with one hand as he fired his space blaster with the other.

"Stop them!" The booming order turned more heads our way, and Isaak released his hold to shoot at two more red armband guys who were running toward his ship from the opposite direction, trying to cut us off.

"Hurry!"

Isaak didn't need to shout. I was sprinting as fast as I could. The floor was diamond hard and grooved, the sharp little peaks cutting painfully into my bare feet.

A large, fur-covered creature lunged for me from the side, and I swung the titan stick hard, right into his face. He screeched like a wounded cat and fell a few steps back. He was on his feet again in seconds, closing in. But slow. Too slow to catch us.

"Move! Move! Move!"

I bolted toward Isaak's voice, waving the stick around in the way he told me not to minutes ago. He was nearly to the ramp that would take us up inside his ship when another alien, this one easily seven feet tall and dark blue, stepped out from behind another spaceship to block our path. It wasn't the Ulza female... but a relative? Definitely the same species of... blue.

"Get out of my way, Graig," Isaak warned, weapon pointed at his chest.

The blue guy grinned. He wasn't hideous, was attractive in a blue kind of way. And he and Isaak seemed to know one another. Maybe he *wasn't* a bad guy? "Not this time, Trion," the blue guy countered, then pointed at me with a strangely long finger. "I want the female."

Isaak shook his head. "She's not for sale."

"I'm taking not buying."

Taking? Yeah, that had already happened. Not once, but twice. Third time was *not* going to be the charm here.

Nope. Blue was totally bad, and I wasn't letting him take me. Something inside me snapped. Broke. I'd heard of a blackout rage, but I'd never felt this before. I didn't care if I lived or died, I was going to hurt the blue asshole standing in my way of escape. I was done with this shit. This was like me with PMS, and someone was keeping me away from chocolate. Sooo not happening.

With what felt like a war cry escaping my chest, I raced at the huge blue alien. He stared for a moment, uncertain how to respond. By the time he snapped out of his shock, I had the titan stick between his ankles. I swung up for his balls. Hard. I had to assume blue guys had balls.

His bellow of pain was much more satisfying than hairy cat-man's had been. Yeah, he had balls, but that didn't mean I wanted to stay around and see them or how he reacted to then being shoved up into his throat.

Isaak blinked in shock at what I'd done, looked from Graig, moaning in a fetal position on the ground, to me. I wasn't sure what to expect, but his wide eyes and cute as hell grin had me grinning back. Yeah, I had rage issues.

"Nice one, *gara*."

"*Z, Isaak. Z for Zara*," I said on a sigh. Men never learned.

I swung my titan stick at the hobbling cat-man who

had stupidly decided to try to grab me again, which made me realize just because these aliens could walk on two legs didn't mean they had any brains.

I burst out laughing—hysterical, crazy laughter—at my ridiculous thought as Isaak spun around and shot down the closer of the two huge Cerberus guys. He fell like a log, the thud causing a group of smaller, not nearly as dangerous looking thugs, to slow completely then stop. Since they didn't have the arm bands, they probably came to the conclusion this wasn't their fight nor worth dying over.

Only one bad guy was left, and the way his face was contorted with rage, he was really angry at Isaak for taking down his friend. Isaak fired, right into his chest, but the guy was not going down. Shit. Should I help?

"Get on the ship!" Isaak's order had my feet moving before I could process the thought, and I raced up the ramp...

Straight into the blue bitch. I bounced back a step or two then dodged her claw-like excuse for fingernails grazing my upper arm as she tried to grab me.

"You're coming with me, female," she snarled. I knew to be wary of pissed off females. She was more dangerous than all the males I'd encountered so far, I was sure.

"No, I'm not," I told her. No fucking way.

She grabbed for me, for my neck. "Give it to me!"

I spun as she grabbed a handful of my hair and pulled me in closer, where she could get her hands on my body.

Wincing in pain from the hair pull, I swung the titan stick up and back, stabbing her in what I hoped was her ribs. "No!"

She grunted but didn't let go. What was she wearing, a bullet proof vest? Zap proof?

Shit. Desperate now, I pulled the weapon forward and struck again, aiming higher.

"Ah!"

Fuck, yes. I got her in the face. I hoped I hit her eye, but I wasn't sure where I'd managed to strike, only that she'd released her hold, and I could move.

I swung around, whipping the stick with me and brought it down across the side of her head. She screamed this time and stumbled, barely standing. Lifting my left foot, I kicked her ass down the ramp and hoped she fell off. I didn't want to have to drag her from the ramp, so we could close it, and she definitely wasn't coming with us.

A guy jumped over her rolling body like a hurdler and landed in a crouch in front of me. Jesus, how many of them were there? Panicked, I brought the titan stick up to strike my new enemy.

"*Gara. It's me.*"

His voice penetrated, and I held still, regained control of myself, even as I watched Ulza roll and fall off the end of the platform.

"I got rid of your blue friend," I told him, taking a deep breath.

Isaak had his hand up, toward me, apparently to ward off a stick attack, but he risked looking back over his shoulder. "Excellent."

He stood and placed his palm on some kind of scanner. Immediately, the loading platform began to retract, the pieces sliding inside one another like an old-fashioned spyglass. The Cerberus bad guy who Isaak had been shooting at when I ran onto the ship appeared. Either Isaak was a horrible shot, or he had some kind of bulletproof vest like Ulza. Or whatever it was called in space. I had to give the guy points for perseverance, for he must have leaped to grab onto the edge, his fingers curled around the platform, hanging on like a monkey.

"*Gara,* can you take care of that? I need to start the engine." Isaak dipped his chin in a pointed reference to my still crackling titan stick.

I glanced from the stick to the asshole trying to pull his elbows up onto the platform. "I can do that."

Isaak took off down a small corridor at a dead run, putting his faith in me to take care of the pesky guy. I raised the titan stick, walked slowly toward the exposed hands grasping for purchase on the ever-shrinking ramp.

I swung once.

His hand disappeared.

Twice.

He lost his grip, but hand number one had returned.

"You asshole. I am not..."

Slam.

"Going..."

Slam.

"With you!"

The ship lurched beneath my feet as I slammed the stick down on the attacker's hand for the last time. He fell with a bellow of rage, and I stood at the door, watching until it was completely sealed, making sure no more thugs needed a titan stick up their ass.

6

"TIME TO GO!"

Isaak's shout had me moving. I dropped the titan stick
—no way was it fitting down the narrow corridor without
accidentally electrocuting myself—and hustled in the
direction of his voice.

I found the cockpit or whatever it was called in a
spaceship. It was literally just like *Star Wars* with two
seats and a shit-ton of buttons and dials and slider things.
I settled into the empty seat beside him.

"Buckle up," he said, not offering me a glance.

I heard and felt the hum of the engine as I clipped
into the five-point harness.

He turned his head, narrowed his eyes as he took me
in from head to breast, his gaze stalling for a second.

I was in a tight, ugly brown outfit which was far from flattering, but it also didn't do anything to hide my hard nipples adorned with gold rings with a gold chain connecting them. I'd heard guys got hard-ons in battle. I got hard nipples. Sue me.

I arched a brow which broke him from his stare.

"Hang on," he said.

I figured he meant that figuratively since there wasn't anything to hang on to, but the second that weird force field disappeared, Isaak hit the gas and shot us past it.

Then he slammed on the brakes, and my head whipped forward.

There was a secondary force field, which I had to guess put us into an air lock or something. That one finally opened, and he *really* hit the gas.

My head shot back, and I felt pressed into the seat as if I were in a ridiculous roller coaster at an amusement park. This one hopefully didn't have a sick drop.

"Holy shit," I muttered, then relaxed when the speed and the craft leveled out. I was glad I never got car sick. "That's got some kick."

I saw his grin, the obvious pride in his ship. He was right. It might be small, but it was fucking fast.

I didn't say anything for several minutes as he maneuvered us past what I thought was an asteroid field. He then pushed some button that I assumed was hyperdrive or turbo-whatever as we were out of there. If we were in a car, I'd have looked over my shoulder to see if they were still following, but I didn't think anyone could have.

He unhooked his restraints and turned to face me.

"All right, *gara*. Who the—" His gaze dropped from mine to my upper arm. "What the *fark* happened to you?"

I looked down, saw the blood staining my top. I hadn't even known I'd been hurt, but now that he'd pointed it out, it stung like a bitch. "That blue lady needs a serious manicure."

He hopped up, loomed over me and released my fancy seat belt. Taking my hand, he led me out of the cockpit and into an ancillary room. I looked around. The craft reminded me of a corporate jet although round and ridiculously fast. In space and not between Omaha and Miami. It was fine for one person, cozy for two. Painful for more than that. There was a tiny bed, unmade, a table the size of a cookie sheet and a bunch of wall cabinets.

He pushed me, so I sat on the bed and opened one of the cabinets, pulling out a wand of some kind. A blue light came on, and he waved it over my arm. The pain receded within seconds.

"What is that thing?" I asked, staring at it then up at him, realizing his face was inches from mine. How had I missed his five o'clock shadow before?

"ReGen wand. Better?"

I nodded.

He turned to the wall again and punched some buttons on what looked like a strange microwave. He looked to me, studied me, then back to the machine. He opened a little door and pulled out some folded clothes. "Here. I hope these fit. I guessed."

I stared at the offering in his hands. "You cooked clothes?"

He frowned then shrugged. "Of course. The S-Gen

61

machine will make whatever you need. How do you get clothes on Earth?"

"I order them online. Or go to the mall."

He frowned some more. "I don't know this mall."

I took the items he held, set them on the bed. A black pair of pants and top. I stood up to change, but he just stood there. Stared. I spun my finger in a circle. "Privacy?"

The corner of his mouth tipped up. "Not much of that on this craft." Still, he turned around, crossed his arms over his chest and leaned against the wall.

"Shouldn't someone be flying this thing?" I asked, tugging off my bloodstained shirt and staring at my arm where Ulza had grabbed me. There was blood but no cut. That wand-thing had healed me. Amazing.

"Automated," he said. "We're good in this area of space. Want to tell me why Cerberus is after you?"

I frowned at his back then slipped the shirt on. It was soft and looser than the drab outfit I'd been given on Trion. I wasn't sure if there were bras in space, but I was thankful I wasn't well endowed because I wasn't going to ask Isaak to make me one for my B cups.

"I don't even know who Cerberus is," I replied. "I told you, I was matched to Trion, and my mate was murdered."

I shucked the old pants, donned the new ones. Without panties.

"You said Bertok killed him." He hadn't moved while I changed.

"That's right. At first, I thought he did it because he wanted me for himself. That guy doesn't have high regard for women," I grumbled.

I heard Isaak's laugh. "Women on Trion are to be cherished and revered. And submissive."

It was my turn to laugh. "Well, I think the testing was wrong then," I told him. "I'm far from submissive." I figured Isaak had probably already realized that after our crazy getaway. "Got any shoes?"

He turned, looked down at my bare feet, then slowly worked up my body. I felt that stare as if it were a caress.

A funny sound escaped his lips as he turned back to the magical machine. Within seconds, he handed me socks and sturdy boots like his own.

My eyes widened, and I couldn't help but stare. "Wow. Thanks." I dropped back onto the bed, put them on. "What about you, space pirate?" I asked, tugging up a sock.

"What about me?"

I glanced up at him. "Why were you under the dome?"

"I kill Hive, take their integrations and sell them."

"Why?"

His broad shoulders went up in a quick shrug. "Credits. Why else?"

"Yet you're from Trion."

"And you're from Earth."

I pursed my lips, looked away and put on the other sock.

"Got a space mansion somewhere?" I asked. "A secret hideaway? Bat cave?"

"You're riding in it."

I sat up, looked around. It wasn't fancy, that was for sure. But it had definitely done the job and got us off that hell hole. I wasn't going to complain. Since it was my first spaceship, I had nothing to compare it to.

"You mentioned something about Ulza, the wicked witch of the west—although she's blue instead of green—taking credits back?"

He leaned against the wall and slid down it, so his butt was on the floor, his knees bent up before him, his wrists resting on them. Since I was on the bed, the only other place to sit was the floor. We were more eye level than before. "Ulza was my primary buyer. I sold her some Hive integration pieces right before I heard about you. Once I helped you escape, she retracted the credits."

"That sucks. She shouldn't be able to do that. Can't you complain to the bank? Or whoever you aliens use to hold your money."

"Banks? We don't use banks. Not for hundreds of years. Too much power in one place, too much corruption. We exchange credits in a free market system."

"So what, you're like Bitcoin all grown up?"

He shook his head, his gaze oddly intense. "You say such strange things. We trade in credits. The payment systems are maintained by the Interstellar Coalition of Planets. Every planet answers to Prillon Prime if they do not maintain the security of the credit system on their planet."

More than I needed to know, but I was sorry to hear that he'd been screwed out of his money. "I'm sorry you lost your money, but I'm glad you helped me. Thank you."

He lifted a hand to rub the back of his neck. "There was no other option. During my transaction with Ulza, I heard about a human female being under the dome." He was quiet for a second then added, "I finally had enough to buy an upgraded ion cannon."

"That sounds big," I said, not sure how to compliment him. The only cannons I knew about were on pirate ships or shooting out T-shirts at sporting events. But… if he was a space pirate, then I had to go with the first.

He turned his head, looked at me. "Not big, but powerful. One shot could destroy an entire asteroid field while traveling at high speed. The targeting software is supposed to be able to lock onto cloaked Hive vessels as well. Take them out."

He sounded like an Earth guy talking about a muscle car.

"Wow," I replied, not having a clue about most of what he's said.

His eagerness at the man-toy slipped away as he sighed. "I gave her three months' worth of Hive tech. For nothing. Now she's not going to do any kind of business with me. Instead, she'll most likely shoot me."

"Yeah, sorry about that," I replied.

"I should spank your ass like I would a misbehaved Trion female."

Um, what? My eyes narrowed at his words. "*Misbehaved?* I didn't ask you to help me. Hell, I was doing pretty darn fine on my own back there." I cocked a thumb over my shoulder. "I saved your ass as much as you saved mine. You can spank my ass because it gets your cock hard but not for anything else."

His eyes widened, and he stayed quiet, which made me more uncomfortable than if he bickered back. With a dinner plate sized hand, he reached out and took hold of my wrist, yanked me off the bed and to my knees beside him. Grabbing my waist, he lifted me up and over his lap, so I straddled him, my body cradled between his sturdy torso and his powerful thighs.

"The idea of spanking you makes my cock hard. I don't have to be doing it to be in such a state," he countered, and I felt the hard length of him against my pussy. His gaze dropped to my breasts and chain linking them. "The idea gets you hot, too."

"It's cold in here," I countered. *Traitorous nipples.*

He tipped his head back and laughed. "Are you always so argumentative?"

"When someone calls me bad," I countered without hesitation.

With a surprisingly gentle touch, he stroked my hair back from my face, his thumb brushing over my cheek.

"You were matched to Trion as an Interstellar Bride, which makes you a Trion female. While you may not think you are submissive, and your behavior certainly shows you otherwise, the testing isn't wrong. You want someone to dominate you, to take control, to allow you to let go of all your troubles, to give them up."

His deep voice made me want to strangle him. It also called to me. I'd been taking care of myself for so long, trusting no one, the idea of sharing a struggle or a burden with another was ridiculously appealing. I'd love to let go of all my troubles. But how? With Isaak?

He was insane.

There was no way I could submit to any male. I didn't trust anyone—not even him. He'd gotten me off Occeron and out of that horrible dome city, but I hadn't even asked where we were going, and that was stupid.

I wasn't going to let him take the upper hand here. He

had to know I wasn't going to go meekly anywhere he wanted. Do anything he said without question. "Give them up? No fucking way."

He arched a brow in denial or... male whatever.

"I don't need a guy to dominate me. I like being on top just fine." With that, I reached down between us, palmed his cock and squeezed. He hissed because that got through loud and clear. I grinned. "I'll show you."

saak

BY THE GODS, this female played with fire. And my cock. But now that I knew the truth, that she had been matched to a male on Trion, I was not fooled by the bravado and challenge in her eyes.

Quite the opposite. I recognized the frantic need for the truth in her gaze. Zara was desperate.

Alone.

Afraid.

She rubbed my cock, and I allowed the touch because I would not deny myself this pleasure. She had something to prove to herself more than me. I knew the truth, and she would soon. First, though, we'd both get the pleasure we craved.

Her lips parted, and I resisted the urge to reach up and rub the plump flesh with a fingertip. I didn't want to touch her lips, I wanted another taste. Now that we were alone and there weren't Cerberus fighters ready to kill, I took what I wanted, claimed her mouth and explored the hot depths. I tasted her fully, took her breath as she touched me, stroking my cock until I groaned.

Too long. I had gone without a female for far too long, and this one? Gods help me, she was too fucking sweet. I didn't dare tell her that, or she'd probably grab my balls instead and rip them off.

Yet she was soft. Defiant. Beautiful.

I hoped her mate found peace in death because I was going to take this female and make her mine. Bury my cock in her core and watch her shudder with pleasure as I filled her. I would make her beg. And scream. And forget who she was. Where she was. Forget everything but me.

Let go.

But not like this. Not until she admitted what she wanted, what she needed... and asked me to give it to her.

Reaching between us, I grabbed her wrists and secured them at her sides. I felt her resistance, her fight. "What are you doing, *gara?*"

She shook her head and twisted her wrists in a half-hearted attempt to break my hold. If she had fought fully, I would release her immediately, but I knew—hoped—that was not what she desired. Not at all.

"Let me go," she hissed, her eyes narrow. Heated. Furious.

"Tell me what you are doing."

Surprisingly, a tear gathered in her eye, slipped down one cheek. Yet she remained stubborn in stony silence. I moved to secure both of her wrists behind her back in just one of my hands and used the other to gently wipe the tear from her cheek.

And just like that, I found the chink in her strength. She'd been through so much since her transport from Earth. More than any female should endure, especially alone.

She was not that way any longer. She didn't need to be so brave. So... strong.

"I will give you anything you desire, *gara*, but only if I know what you need."

She choked back an angry cry and twisted. Hard. Ah, she was not yet ready.

I released her at once, and she scrambled away from me on hands and knees, chest heaving like she'd run a long race. "I don't need anything. I want—"

I waited in silence. I would not take advantage of a female who did not know her own mind. Or couldn't voice her needs aloud. I would not guess with her, and I would not push. She would need to discover it on her own, for it was within her, this need she didn't realize she even had.

What had her life on Earth been like to hide such desired beauty?

She was an Interstellar Bride. Her mate was dead, but she was a true prize, a female who not only longed for the comfort and safety a dominant Trion mate could provide but hungered for him. Needed to surrender control.

She'd volunteered to be matched. The testing had plumbed her subconscious, found her deepest needs and desires. Matched her to Trion, the planet where females were the most submissive in the galaxy.

Zara struggled to her feet and wiped at her eyes,

where I assumed more tears streaked her soft cheeks, tears I could not see. Or perhaps the tears were imagined. Emotional wounds. Invisible to my eye.

Our gazes locked, and I rose slowly as well, not even attempting to hide the bulge of the hard cock in my pants. Proof of my desire. Lust. I had needs of my own, and she was stirring everything primitive within me to a dangerous level. She'd felt it in the palm of her hand. "What do you want, *gara*?" I asked, my voice soft. Soothing.

She used trembling hands to rub both of her arms, as if cold. The ship was anything but sensing our body temperatures and adjusting the environmental controls accordingly.

"Don't call me that," she hissed.

One of these days, she'd preen and be soothed by that endearment, know it was honest and filled with desire.

Taking a step forward, I approached. Another. The room was small, and in moments, I stood toe to toe with the defiant female. Using every bit of tenderness I could summon as my body raged at me to turn her around, shove her against the wall and make her mine, I grazed her chin with my fingertips and angled her face up so our eyes met. Held. "Anything, *gara*. But I do not take what is not freely given."

Her tongue traced a rapid line across her lips and her breathing hitched. A flush heated her cheeks, but she did not pull away. "What do you want me to give you?"

Everything, I realized. I wanted this female to be mine. Her fire and courage, her sass, the flash of defiance in her eyes. More, I wanted her heart and her body and her trust. I had never encountered another female like her, not even Ivy, with her Hive implants and mate, Zenos, by her side. Never had I met a woman, a human woman, who could escape Jirghogis and steal his titan stick, face down Ulza of Cerberus legion, and stand toe-to-toe with a thief and smuggler she barely knew but instinctively trusted not to hurt her.

She was remarkable. One of a kind.

Mine.

"Isaak?" Zara's prompt made me realize I'd been staring. I needed to maintain control. Never had I been so close to giving in to my body's demands for a mate. The need to bury my cock deep drove me with a sharp, knife-edged pain that I welcomed. Embraced. I would ride my need for hours if she would allow me to pleasure her, glory in the fire building in both mind and body until my release was an agony of bliss.

But my desire was built on a lie. Out here in space, I had no home to offer a female. No family name, no riches, no security. I would never take a female into Hive controlled territory on one of my raids. And I could not leave a mate unprotected in this sector of space long enough to go on my own.

I wanted a mate, but I did not deserve one. Not living like I did. If I returned to Trion… there I had everything for a mate, but my parents had made it clear I did not belong. That I was not wanted.

"I want many things, *gara*. But for now, I want you to take off your clothes and let me look at you."

Her lip trembled. "And then what?"

She had not denied me, and that was all the encouragement I needed. "Then I will pleasure you, *gara,* with my hands and my mouth."

Her lips parted and a pink blush darkened her cheeks further. The signs of her interest were visible, but I needed the words. "Is this what you want? I must hear the words."

She blinked, and I could practically see her mind debating her body's desires. "Yes."

Fark, yes. My cock pulsed in my pants, eager to get to her, to get *in* her. I would take her, but I would do it as the Trion male I was. I would dominate. Give her what she needed. Her needs would not be denied, even ones I would have to show her she had.

I cleared my throat, dropped my voice into a deep timbre. "You will obey me while we are in this room. I saw your strength. Your bravery. Here, you do not need to be strong. Or brave. You only need to listen. To obey. To feel. I shall protect you in all ways."

She nodded, and I continued. "Should you disobey, I will spank your bare bottom then fuck you until you scream your pleasure."

She shifted from foot to foot, clenched her thighs together. Would she allow me to touch her? To thrust my fingers into that wet pussy and bring her relief? I'd voiced her desires aloud, and I saw her needy response.

Her gaze darted to the side, where she'd left the titan stick, and I stepped back at once. "Is that what you need to feel safe? A weapon within reach to trust me? If that is the case, I will deny us both what we both truly desire. I will go."

She reached for me, her fingers curling into the fabric of my shirt. That one touch sealed her fate. "No," she whispered then went on, her voice stronger. "I just, I'm

73

sorry. I want you. This. What you said. Here. In this room."

Meaning she would relent to my control in this moment, in this ship. And this ship alone.

"Just no kinky stuff, okay?"

I wrapped my arms around her and pulled her close, as I had longed to do for too long, and held her pressed to me. Nothing more, just held her, comforted her with touch. With the feel of my body, so different from hers. Where I was hard edges and muscled, she was so small, so fragile. So soft. Feminine. Perfect.

Fark.

"What is *kinky* stuff?" I asked, murmuring into her silky hair. "I do not know this term."

She pressed her forehead to my chest as if embarrassed. "You know, no handcuffs. Don't tie me up or beat me with anything or cut me or stick needles in my skin. Electricity. Whips. Stuff like that. I don't like pain."

My body had become more rigid with each word from her mouth. This kinky stuff did not interest me. In fact, it made me furious. Burying my fist in her hair, I angled her face up to mine, so I could look in her eyes. "I do not bring pain, *gara.* Only pleasure."

"You said you'd spank me," she said.

"I also said I would fuck you after until you screamed with pleasure."

Her blue-green eyes met mine, held, as if assessing. "If I say stop, you'll stop?"

"I am a dominant male, not a monster. I do not force myself on a female. Ever."

She shuddered and melted into my arms. *Fark*, it felt perfect, like she was exactly where she belonged. I had never been tested for an Interstellar Bride, but something inside me insisted—despite all logic or odds to the contrary—that if I had, Zara of Earth would have been mine. I hadn't even known she existed when I landed on Occeron earlier, parked my ship in Omega Dome. And now...

"All right." Too soon she pulled away from me but stopped when the backs of her legs bumped against the small sleeping area. Gazes locked, she reached for the hem of her tunic and pulled it off over her head. She'd remembered my initial request to bare herself.

My fingers itched to touch her, my mouth watered to taste. Her skin was pale, creamy. Her breasts were small, yet a handful. Pink nipples were adorned with simple golden rings, the lightweight chain running between her nipples was bare. Her mate had been killed before he could adorn her properly, make her his. If her mate had not adorned her body, then he had not claimed it. I would be the first male to give her her deepest desires.

Around her neck she wore an elaborate golden collar with an oval shaped pendant hanging at the perfect height to form a triangle with her pert nipples. I did not recognize the design and assumed the collar was something personal to her.

If she loved the item, I would allow her to keep it. If not, I would replace that collar with one of my own. One sparkling with jewels and linked to the rings piercing her breasts. I would see the triangle I imagined come to life on her body, make her sparkle like a very well-kept female.

If she were mine, I would adorn her properly.

She looked ripe to be claimed, and I would do that. Claim her.

Licking her lips, it had my cock punching against my pants to get out and have that tongue on it.

"I will do what you say, but shouldn't we have a safe word or something?" Her light hair fell over her bare shoulders in a thick cascade of gold and soft brown.

"A safe word?" I had never heard of such a thing. "What is the purpose of this word? You are safe." I glanced around the ship, wondering what she found to be dangerous.

Her hands crossed her chest in a defensive gesture I immediately hated. "If I say it, no matter what we are doing, you stop. A safe word."

"I see." I had given her my assurance I would not harm her, but she still did not trust me. I did not like it, but I understood. This need for a word gave her some control still although it was tied to what she feared not what she desired. She wasn't denying herself with this... safe word. She was protecting. When she was mine, truly mine, I would make sure she never needed to use such a word. Ever. "Very well. Choose your word, female. I will abide by your choice."

"Hurricane."

I waited a moment for my NPU to process the strange Earth term. "Ah, a storm on your planet."

Her smile made my cock ache. "No, a really amazing drink in New Orleans. I had a few too many at Mardi Gras a couple years ago. I was hungover for two days."

I stepped forward, only understanding about half of what she said, but it was enough. It was the word of her choice, so she felt safe with me. I would not forget, no matter the reason for her selecting it. "Take off the rest of your clothes and place your hands over your head."

She grumbled as she removed her shoes, socks and pants, but I did not interrupt, too eager to see what would soon be mine. When she straightened, still mumbling about this strange beverage, I opened my mouth to interrupt when the sight of a golden bar piercing her naval brought me up short.

I had seen a teasing glimpse of it before, but now... What was the meaning of such a piercing on Earth? Was it a sign she'd been claimed? That she'd belonged to someone there? It couldn't be, for she'd been a bride. Volunteered.

I'd been patient and would be patient still, yet I wanted to taste. I wanted to adorn the golden chain running between her nipples, tug them into tight peaks. The golden bar I wanted to lick. Taste. The sight exotic and unique. This female continued to surprise me, and that alone made my cock harden and pulse. I stepped close, and she turned. I stepped even closer. She might retreat, but I would not give her room. "Hands over your head. Back to the wall. Do not move unless I tell you to."

Her tongue flicked out again, swiped her bottom lip as she bumped into the unforgiving wall. "Okay."

Slowly, I shook my head as I took in every inch of her. Pale skin, shapely hips, trim waist. Upturned nipples. And a pussy that was bare except for pale curls above that all but beckoned me to seek every hidden treasure.

"Yes, master," I said as I visually drank my fill. "You will call me master."

She frowned. "That's kinky."

I thought of her previous description of this term.

Cutting her flesh. Striking her with a whip. Worse. The images enraged me. She would not think of such things with me. "On your hands and knees."

When she hesitated, I easily lifted her in my arms, carried her to the bed and sat down with her stomach across my thighs.

"Hey!" she shouted, kicking and squirming.

With her face down, her round, perfect ass tempted me almost as much as her pussy. "You did not listen to me, *gara*. You did not obey your master's commands."

"What? Oh, I just—"

With a light slap, I brought my hand down on her bottom, expecting her to yell. Squirm. Protest.

She did none of these things.

Instead, she settled, then moaned. "Oh, god."

Fark, just as I'd assumed. She was the perfect Trion female.

The scent of her wet heat permeated the air, and I inhaled sharply, my cock bursting at the seam of my pants. I was hot. Overheated. Holding her in place with one hand, I removed my own tunic, tossed it across the room. Skin. I would have her hands on my skin soon. Her mouth. Her body. Everywhere. I would take her everywhere.

With a sharp swat on her opposite ass cheek, I peppered her bottom with my heated palm until her flesh was a hot pink, and her pussy juices had wet the insides of her thighs. "Before you say anything, this isn't a beating."

"It's punishment," she countered, her hair falling in a curtain around her face.

"It is not punishment if you are aroused by it. That

you can't deny. The punishment comes when I don't allow you to orgasm after."

"Oh God," she moaned, realizing quickly that I didn't need to beat or harm her to have her comply.

"Call me master," I repeated.

I gave her an out, a way to make the spanking stop, but she refused. "No."

Pulling her bottom up into the air, I pushed two fingers deep inside her molten pussy and scissored them inside the tight channel. She bucked, her fingertips digging deeply into the muscles of my legs, but she did not try to move away. I slipped them from the wet heat. She whimpered. "Call me Master."

"No."

Rubbing my thumb along her clit, I found the sensitive flesh and plucked at it like I would a string, over and over until she was a panting, sweaty mess. But I did not allow her to come. Would not allow her to find release until she addressed me properly. "Who am I?"

"Isaak."

My name on her lips brought me pleasure but was still an act of defiance. One my nature would not allow. Not here. Not now, with her naked body on display. She would surrender control. I would not lose this battle. Something told me if I allowed her even a small victory, I would never have the chance to make her truly mine again. She was too defiant. Too strong. She had to learn what was in her, what the testing had discovered she truly desired.

I had to conquer her here and now for that alone. But also because she may never give me another chance. Might choose another male on Trion. A worthy male. A fighter who had served the Coalition Fleet and earned his place by her side. Who would not push her to call him master.

No. I was too damn selfish to allow that. She was mine now. Mine.

"Do you wish to use your safe word?" I asked. She had yet to say it, which meant she was not opposed to the position in which she found herself.

"No."

Reaching below my feet, I pulled a small footstool from beneath the sleeping mat, one just large enough for me to rest both booted feet upon when my legs were stretched out before me.

I lifted my feet and rested my heels on the stool. Legs straight before me and slightly down at an angle, I lifted my female so that she straddled my legs but facing away from me and toward my boots. Her breasts rested against my knees, her stomach covered my thighs, and her thighs wrapped around my hips. I stared down the length of her curves, the delicate line of her spine, the swells of her hips, the spread ass cheeks exposing the wettest, hottest pussy I'd ever seen. I pulled my cock free from the front of my pants. "Place your hands on my ankles, *gara,* and do not move unless I give you permission. Do you understand?"

"Yes." She shuddered at the tone of my voice, the command, her flesh rising in small, sensitive bumps as her body responded to me.

"Yes, Master," I insisted.

She shook her head from side to side and buried her chin between my legs, refusing to answer me. Why this was so difficult for her, I did not know, but it was a battle I would win.

Lifting her hips, I placed my cock at her heated core and pulled her backward, toward me, sliding her onto my hard length like placing a sheath on a sword. She cried out, the delectable sound echoing off the walls of the room. Her inner walls clenched, the heat of her surrounding me. Her arousal coating my cock, dripping onto my balls.

She used her grip on my ankles to press back, trying to take more, to force my pace. But I would not move. Sweat dotted my brow. "No, *gara*. I am not going to fuck you. Not yet. Not until you call me master."

"No."

Cock buried deep, I held completely still as she wiggled her hips. Writhed. Tried to gain position. Friction. Motion. I denied her. And myself.

Sliding my hands down her sides, I reached beneath her and cupped her breasts, found the rings and chain there. Tugged gently when she tried to move away.

"Oh, God." Her groan was accompanied by the walls of her pussy clamping down even more on my cock, and I struggled to control the urge to rut into her body like an animal.

"Not god. I am a male," I clarified. "A dominant Trion male, and you will call me master, or you will not be allowed to come." I tugged gently on the chain between her breasts and used the weight of her body on my forearms to pull her up and back onto my cock, fully penetrating her. My cock hit the hard wall of her womb, and she whimpered, her body flooding mine with even more wet welcome.

"Please."

Ah, she begged.

"Master. Who is your master?" Releasing one nipple, I wrapped a fist in her hair and gently tugged, lifting her face from where she'd been hiding from me, arching her back, fucking her as I held her in place for my cock.

"No one. I just want—"

I thrust. Hard. "Who is your master?"

"I don't have a—"

Rocking my hips up and forward beneath her, I rubbed the fabric of my pants that had gathered into a hard fold at the base of my cock against her clit.

"Ahhh!" The first tremor of her orgasm gripped my cock, and I stopped. Everything. I let her go. Pulled her off my cock which I was sure was as excruciating for me as it was for her. Released her from my arms and placed her gently on the floor. When she rolled onto her side with a whimper, it took every ounce of power and discipline I had not to give in, to roll her onto her back and plunge deep, to take what I knew she would give me.

But I did not want a quick fuck. Despite the gods and fate and every other damn thing in the universe, I wanted her to be mine. I would not fail her by being weak when she needed me to be stronger than I'd ever been before. She would know I would not falter, would not give in. I would give her everything... in trade for her submission.

"Isaak! That was mean."

"I am not Isaak." I walked to a flat section of the wall and opened a small compartment, my cock hard and long, coated in her juices. The head was flared and angry, pre-cum seeping from it like a faucet.

I went to the S-gen machine, ordered up what I

wanted. I considered the use of the Prillon training device on her perfect ass. I would generate one of those... for later.

For now...

Rolling her onto her back, I was pleased when she did not resist. She did not use her safe word. I couldn't help but smile at my defiant, submissive one. She didn't realize that in her refusal to say her special word that she was submitting. Not well, but she was nonetheless. I refused to tell her that, for I had no doubt she'd call it then, just out of spite alone.

"Call me Master."

She shook her head, her long hair a tangle on the floor behind her. "No way. Sorry. The sex might be great, but—"

I squatted down beside her and attached the device to one nipple ring, and she glanced down, confused. "What is that?"

The second went on her opposite ring before she had finished the question. And then I gently moved her thighs apart and attached the third to her clit. Admiring my work, wishing I had true chains and adornments to drape all over her beautiful curves—and the Trion right to do so—I slid the control device onto my finger and walked to the door, stripping my pants as I went. When I reached the far side of the room, I turned and stood with my back to the only exit. She had come up onto her knees but looked down at her piercings and the small device I had attached to her clit. No doubt they felt heavy, even without me activating the devices I'd attached. Although there was nowhere for her to go on the ship. No retreat. Her only escape was the one word. Hurricane.

"Come to me, *gara*. Come to your master and kneel."

She tilted her head to the side as if I had confused her. She looked so delicate and soft. So vulnerable. Naked. Mine. Not forever but for now, she was mine.

"Do I need to say the word? Because you are getting weirder and—"

I activated the control on my finger, and she cried out, dropping to her hands and knees as the devices I had placed on her erogenous zones came to life. When she lifted her head to gaze up at me with wide, aroused eyes, when it looked like she would speak, I turned up the power and watched her roll onto her side, her head thrown back, hands clasped over her breasts as she moaned with pleasure. Her hips writhed.

"Oh, God."

I turned them off. "Not a god. A dominant Trion male and your master."

"Holy shit." She craned her neck to look at me, and I recognized the fire in her gaze. The defiance. "I just wanted to feel good for a few minutes. I don't need this whole Dom-sub game you are playing."

I activated the device. Again. And again. Never allowing her to come. Just building her higher and higher into her pleasure until I had no doubt she'd come all over my cock the instant I sank inside her. A sheen of sweat coated her skin, her body was flushed, her nipples tight. Her pussy lips, which I caught a glimpse of every time she shifted and squirmed, were dark and swollen.

"This is not a game. Your pleasure is mine. Your orgasms are mine. Your body is mine. I am your master."

8

I was going to kill him. Or fuck him. Or lick him all over.

If I could get close enough before he sent another delicious zing through my entire body like lightning to my nipples and my clit. I was on the edge, had been for too long, since he pushed that huge cock inside me... then did nothing.

I ached. I needed to come. Not just wanted. Not turned on, fired up, whatever. My body was in full-on revolt. If I thought he would let me, I would reach downtown and take care of my orgasm myself.

Sliding my hands low to try, I wasn't even close when he zapped me again. My eyes rolled into the back of my fucking head, and I moaned.

I could say *hurricane,* and it would stop. But did I want

it to stop? No. Hell, no. But I wanted to come, and the only way that was going to happen was if he allowed my release.

Allowed me. How had I sunk to that?

The bliss pulsed through me, my clit so big and hard I bucked my hips up as if trying to rub it against air. How could something feel so good and so bad at the same time? What was wrong with me? My ass still stung from the spanking, and I had caught myself rubbing it against the floor to wake up the sting. I wanted more. Wanted him to spank my ass with his fingers buried in my pussy again until I came all over him, ass in the air. Screaming.

Please. *Please.*

He was fucking ripped, muscles and scars and power, like a god standing at the door with his toys and his eyes so hot they burned my skin every time he looked at me. His pants were gone, and his big cock jutted out. It was a reminder that I wasn't the only one affected here. I knew no guy who pulled out and walked away once he'd gotten his dick buried deep. His hard length was a dark plum color, the head like a huge ass fire helmet. Pre-cum slipped down it, and I wanted to taste it, to flick it off.

I wanted to say it. *Master.* One stupid word shouldn't be so hard to say. It was just sex. A game.

Except this was no game, and somehow, deep down, I knew that if I said the word, I'd be in deep, deep trouble.

Yet I hadn't used my safe word. End this one way or the other. I could say it and be done. I'd win.

And then what? Would I win? It seemed the only way to have a winner was if I said the words, and he fucked me. We'd both win, both get the orgasm we both needed like air.

If the safe word came from my lips, I'd still want more, and he'd dump me on Trion. Turn me over to some other Trion male who wanted me to call *him* master? Or worse, I'd go home to Earth and hook up with some loser who could barely pull his head away from his phone long enough to kiss me a couple times before getting himself off?

Isaak was standing there, cock hard and balls probably bluer than Ulza the wicked witch's skin. He wasn't taking. Well, he wanted me to call him master, but he was giving. Giving me pleasure. Showing me how I could feel if I just gave over. I'd get what I wanted. His cock. An orgasm.

But only then would he get his pleasure, too.

Damn it. Fuck. Frustration built inside me like steam in a tea kettle, and I was about to blow.

"Call me master," he said once more.

I shook my head. "No."

He studied me for long minutes that felt like an hour as I laid on the floor looking up at him, admiring his chest. His dark hair. The cut of his jaw. The thick cock that jutted heavily from between his powerful legs. He really was gorgeous. I wanted to kiss him again. I wanted his arms around me. I wanted to feel safe and treasured and... safe.

"I see. Perhaps you require a different sort of persuasion."

If I had the energy left, I would have rolled my eyes at the dramatic statement, but the truth was, I didn't. Every cell and fiber of my being was focused on holding onto the pleasure that was drifting away like clouds in the wind leaving me cold and lonely.

Again.

I blinked, and he was next to me, lifting me onto his lap, but this time I faced him, straddled his hips, and his cock slid inside my wet core like we'd been made for one another. I cried out at the feel of him once again stretching me open, filling me up.

"You will eventually call me master, Zara. You will surrender."

"No." I denied him even as his cock slipped deeper, striking my womb.

"I will earn your trust, *gara*. I demanded too much, too soon, as is my nature. But I will learn what you need, and you will surrender."

Afraid he was right, I didn't deny his words. Instead, I reached for his hair and pulled his lips to mine for a soul-crushing kiss.

I shifted my hips, riding him, trying to take what I needed. He wrapped his hands around me, crushing me to his chest, restricting my movement. I nearly sobbed in frustration. My nipples caressed by the stroke of skin on skin as our chests met. I felt him move oddly, and the devices activated once more.

With his cock buried deep, I screamed as the orgasm instantly rolled over me like a tank crushing a daisy. One. Then two. The aftershocks were so strong they led to a third, and he hadn't even moved. He held my head in his hands, tilted my face to his, and held my gaze as my body became something else, not mine.

His.

When I was too weak to do anything but collapse against his chest, he groaned, hands fisted in my hair, holding me tightly as his cock jumped, and he found his own release, his seed coating my core with heat and a ridiculous possessiveness I had never felt before.

His scent filled my head with warmth. Safety. Contentment. I relaxed in his arms, and he stroked my sweaty back like I was precious. Special. Safe. The illusion, if it were one, was too damn good to dismiss, so I stayed where I was, content to play pretend for as long as we could.

I hadn't said my safe word. Yet I hadn't said the word he wanted either. We'd both given in.

Still, maybe I could somehow be his. Maybe. But maybe, he could be mine, too.

My Master.

————

Isaak

ZARA SPRAWLED ATOP ME, her body pliant and soft. Whether she knew it or not, she trusted me. No one would sleep so deeply otherwise. She was soft and warm, pliant and... sweet in my arms.

The fact made my chest ache with a strange longing I hadn't felt in years, and I looked away from the beautiful, feisty female in my arms and stared at the dark ceiling, watched the ship's lights blink on and off as it went about the business of traveling through space. For too long, I'd slept in this room alone. Stared up just as I was now but not seen it. Not seen anything around me but blood and Hive and what I was willing to risk to feel something.

I inhaled deeply. Zara did not smell like flowers or

sweets. She smelled like me—and sex—and I found that extremely satisfying.

If I didn't get ahold of myself, I'd be adorning her with more jewels than her tender flesh could hold.

Not that she'd allow my claim. Not yet. What we'd just shared was a start, showed it was possible but would take effort. Cajoling. Trust. I still had time.

"*Proximity warning,*" the auto-voice warned. "*Automatic shielding activated. Proximity warning. Automatic shielding activated.*"

What the—?

"Brace for impact in five, four, three—"

I wrapped my arm around Zara and grabbed the stabilizer bar above my head with the other. My feet I shoved into the padded side pockets built into the bed frame for just this purpose.

"What's going on?" Zara blinked at me. Sleepy. Confused.

"Two, one—"

"Hold onto me," I ordered. Thank the gods Zara didn't ask questions, simply wrapped her arms and legs around my torso and clung.

"Impact." The ship's artificial intelligence sounded like a grumpy old space captain. I could have chosen from dozens of voices, but I didn't want the soft sound of a female surrounding me when I was about to kill Hive or deal with people like Ulza.

The ship rocked and a loud explosion boomed through the ship, shaking everything. My body strained to hold both my weight and Zara's as the ship tilted, flipping onto its side before righting itself.

"What the hell?" Zara looked at me as I gently dropped her back onto the bed as I stood.

"We're under attack." I tugged up my pants and shoved my cock within. If someone was coming after us, I didn't want my ass hanging out.

"From who?"

I looked at her, at her creamy skin and silken hair and very human beauty, and I told her the truth. "I don't know. Cerberus is probably angry you got away, but I doubt they'd come this far to get you back." I spun on my heel and ran to the door. Motion behind me had me turning my head to find Zara climbing quickly out of bed as well. I stopped her with a held-up hand.

"No. Stay here."

Another impact shook the ship, and I slapped my palm against the wall. I ran out into the corridor and headed straight for the pilot's chair.

I wasn't surprised when Zara sat her naked ass in the seat next to me. "I'm not staying back there. I can help." She tucked her long hair behind her ear. "Tell me what to do."

Fark. "Buckle those straps, so I don't have to worry about you. And sit still."

"Okay." She reached for the straps, pulled them over her head and around her curves, the tight fit making her breasts jut out at a perfect angle. I didn't miss the glitter of the gold rings and chain from the cockpit's lights.

"*Proximity alert. Automatic shielding at sixty percent.*" The ship's gruff voice barked at me as if I were an idiot for not moving faster.

Shirtless and my pants open in my own chair, I

buckled the straps and punched a button to activate a set of pre-programmed evasive maneuvers that had outsmarted more than one Hive Scout ship in the past. Unless there were multiple ships attacking us, which was completely ridiculous in this sector of space, this should—

"Brace for impact in five, four, three, two, one...impact."

Fark. The ship shuddered and another loud boom sounded.

Zara ducked her head instinctively although it would do nothing to protect her. "Who is shooting at us?"

"Ask the ship." I punched in a code to reroute more power to the shields, which were down to fifty percent.

"Ship, who is shooting at us?" Zara talked to the air in an innocent way that made me want to kiss her. Again. I assumed they didn't have voice activated ships on Earth.

We were being attacked, we were naked—I was mostly, and Zara was completely—and I was smiling. Either I was going insane, or Zara was some kind of miracle. "The ship's name is Shadow."

She looked to me, arched her pale eyebrow in question. When I didn't reply, she asked, "Shadow, who is shooting at us?"

"Zara of Earth, I do not recognize your authority to—" My ship was an ass.

"It knows who I am?" Zara's eyes widened.

"Shadow, respond to Zara," I commanded. "Authorization Isaak nine seven Trion echo three."

"Acknowledged." The ship's system processed my order to allow Zara access to commands. *"We are being pursued by a stealth class, Spectra Five ship with Cerberus Legion coding."*

"Uh oh. That sounds like the blue lady is still really mad about the whole titan stick incident." Zara laughed. "I should have shoved it up her ass."

My hand froze on the way to the weapons panel, and I had to blink twice. Hard. I was not used to a female who spoke in such a way, even if it was something I wanted to do myself. I activated my ion cannon. It wasn't the Spectra IV ion cannon, but whoever was chasing us wasn't going to like it. "Shadow, light 'em up."

"Shooting to kill, Captain." I heard the sounds of the blasters, but the structural stabilizers minimized the vibrations.

Zara turned to look at me. "What did he just say?"

It was my turn to laugh. "I did a bit of specialty programming." I watched with great satisfaction as the ship which had been following us disengaged and a few seconds later disappeared from radar. "Hunting Hive ships can be intense. I couldn't stand all of the official language and protocol."

Zara smiled at me as she inspected every inch of my bare body.

"Proximity alert cancelled. They are running scared. Should I pursue?"

Normally, if we were hunting Hive, I would say yes. Hive parts were my livelihood, and I couldn't normally let them get away. But this time, I was the one being hunted. Or, rather, Zara was. It sure as *fark* wasn't me. And I didn't care for the feeling of being prey. "Negative. Get us to Transport Station Zenith as fast as you can."

"Lighting my ass on fire, Captain."

I checked the readings for damage, relieved to find

there was little to none from the surprise attack. My ship was small but heavily armored and fast as they came.

"They'll be back, won't they?" she asked, glancing out the window as if she could see the craft that had been attacking.

I leaned back and unhooked my straps. Zara did the same. When she was free of the restraints, I stood and lifted her to her feet to stand before me. Her breasts with those small gold hoops and chain were right in front of my face. *Fark.*

"Who are you?"

She frowned. "I already told you."

Slowly, I shook my head. "No. Who are you? Why are you being followed? You're not just an Interstellar Bride. You can't be. What does Cerberus Legion want from you?"

It made no sense. A female who'd only arrived in space was wanted—and chased—by Cerberus legion from Rogue 5.

"I have no idea."

Tilting her head up so I could look directly into her eyes, I asked again. "Zara, no female is worth this much trouble. Even a female from Earth wouldn't be worth the fuel and the missiles they fired at my ship. What aren't you telling me?"

She shook her head before I finished speaking. "I swear, I have no idea. I signed up to be an Interstellar Bride, to get out of the shitshow that my life had turned into. I took the test, woke up on Trion, and Bertok was there, waiting to kill my mate. That's all I know."

She seemed sincere, but something wasn't right.

"What about your life on Earth? Are you royal? Would they want to ransom you to a wealthy family?"

That made her grunt with apparent disdain then begin to laugh. "God, could you imagine?" she asked although it seemed to be a rhetorical question, so I remained quiet. "I grew up poor, Isaak. Ghetto. We never had money. I didn't go to college. My neighborhood was run by gangs and drug dealers. Even the cops steered clear. I'm not special. I'm nobody."

The finality of her words, the absolute conviction behind them made me angry. "You are Zara of Trion. You are strong and fearless and beautiful." And mine. I fought with myself not to speak the last two words aloud. I could not make promises I knew I could not keep. She had shared her body with me but had not surrendered her heart, and that was for the best.

No matter that everything within me hated the knowing. Wanted not just her heart but her soul. Everything. I wanted everything.

Guess my father had been right. I was just a selfish bastard after all. I had nothing to offer this beautiful female. Nothing. I shouldn't even be touching her, *fark,* speaking to her. She was well out of my reach.

Telling my conscience to shut up, I pulled her close and wrapped my arms around her. She shivered and melted into the warmth I offered. While I liked her bare, the ship wasn't thermally set to her small body. The adrenaline of the chase was wearing off, but I had never experienced the withdrawal bare.

"What now?" she asked.

"Now we go to Transport Station Zenith and meet with Ivy and Zenos."

"Are they your friends?"

"Ivy is from Earth, like you. And Zenos is from Rogue 5. Astra legion. They have no love for Cerberus. If anyone can figure out what might be going on, it's those two."

ara, Canteen, Transport Station Zenith, Sector 437

"Do people grow taller in space because of less gravity or something?" I asked as another giant passed, my sense of humor firmly in place. We'd arrived at this new place, a transport station Isaak informed me, parked the spaceship and were supposed to go directly to what sounded like a regular, old-fashioned bar. Canteen it was called. Whatever. Isaak promised me they served drinks. Food. People came from all over. He also swore there would be more uniforms and less... blue.

"Atlan." His one-word answer had me turning around to stare. So, that was one of the beasts I'd heard about. I'd seen the other one on television, on that alien bachelor show. But somehow, the true size of that one hadn't quite made it through the TV screen.

"Holy crap. He's huge." And hot. Wisely, I kept the second part of my opinion to myself.

Isaak chuckled. "You should see their cousins, the Forsians. Even bigger."

He was holding my hand—my other held my titan stick—and every time a big, bad alien passed, he pulled me closer and a bit behind him. I didn't even think he noticed, but it was...sweet. I was used to looking out for myself, but I wasn't going to complain. Not after Bertok murdering my mate, the blue lady, the getaway, the orgasms, and the shoot-out in space. I had taken a bit of a nap on Isaak's ship, but to be honest, my nerves were fried. Besides, it was nice to let someone else take the lead for once. Not that I had plans to get used to it. Isaak had made it very clear that he was taking me to Ivy—an Earth girl—and that would be the end of it. I was going back to Trion. Isaak was not.

End. Of. Discussion.

Isaak had his gun strapped to his thigh, but he was relaxed. Maybe his calm was the result of all that hot sex. Whatever the reason, he didn't seem too concerned about being shot at or chased. Although after the whole attack in space situation, I needed another orgasm or two to calm down. I'd been in fights at home. Hell, I'd even fought it out under The Omega Dome and stabbed the scaly, poisonous lizard man with his own cattle prod. But a shootout in space? Naked?

Never.

Take that, *Star Trek*.

I'd never been in a shootout quite like that before, but I'd seen them on TV. Not one had it where the actors were bare assed. As for Isaak's fine body and big cock, he was impressive, and he could walk around with everything on display for all I cared. The man should be proud of what he was packing—and I wasn't talking about the gun in his thigh holster—and want to show it off.

I followed Isaak down a long corridor, this one much cleaner than the one I'd run down in the dome. Here, the air didn't smell like unwashed bodies, animals and nasty body fluids. The walls were metallic and shiny, the results, no doubt, of the odd circular robotic creatures that stuck to the walls like snails inside a fish tank. They had rotating brushes that looked like half mop, half broom, and left a pleasant, fresh air kind of smell behind. Walking up and down the halls were mostly males, huge males of various races I'd not seen before. Some had fangs, some wore black and gray armor with the Coalition Fleet insignia I recognized from my time at the Interstellar Brides processing center. Some, like Isaak, just walked around like they owned the place.

Some looked human, but I wasn't fooled. Even if they looked like us, I knew damn good and well these males were not men. They were aliens. Tall, bulging muscles, intense stares and almost every single one noticed me before Isaak. Their eyes would flash from my breasts— where the nipple rings and chain were clearly visible through the tunic Isaak had given me—to the collar around my neck. Satisfied, they did the man thing— lifting their chin or tilting their head at Isaak—to let him know they had assessed the situation with the female and would not interfere.

Like I wasn't even there.

At first, I hated them all. Then I decided I didn't mind

their assessment. If it had been Bertok dragging me along, or the blue lady, I would have more than welcomed some hot alien interference.

Isaak would tell me their species after they passed—and after I had asked him about twenty times in a row. Viken. Prillon. Atlan...and boy oh boy, those boys were big. There were Hunters, whatever that was, and then there were the gangsters from Rogue 5. I stopped asking about them. Every single one of them looked different—hybrids, Isaak informed me—and they all wore arm bands. Different colors but easy to see. Steer clear, that was my policy when it came to those creeps.

Yep. I was still in space on some kind of gigantic, floating space station in the middle of nowhere. I had no clue where we were other than the name, so I had to trust him that we were safe. That the chasing and shooting was over. And that there really would be a woman from Earth at the end of this walk.

The canteen doors were three times the size I was used to back home, but when two of the Coalition guys walked through, side-by-side, I realized the size was a necessity.

"Prillons."

"They mate in pairs, right?" That's what Warden Egara and the pamphlets back at the bride testing center had informed me. Two of them. One woman.

Wow. That was a lot of man. Or alien.

"Jealous, *gara*? Did I not satisfy your needs?" He pulled me to the side of the large doors and turned me to face him as more aliens passed. His dark hair was a little wild, but that seemed to be normal for him and not just a post-sex look. He lifted his free hand and wrapped the base of my neck in his warm, firm grip. God, the things that one simple touch made me feel.

"You know you did." My pussy clenched, further reminding me that I got hot for things I'd never expected. Domination. Edging. Safe words.

But those things didn't make a relationship. They made sex hot as hell. Who knew?

Isaak, apparently. He was from Trion. Were all males from Trion like him? If my matched mate had lived, would he have done the same things to me? Made me call him master? Made me writhe and sweat and want to beg?

Did I respond to Isaak that way because he helped save my life? Or were my brain and body somehow hardwired to want a firm twist of his hand in my hair? A rough kiss?

Isaak pulled me to him and kissed me as if he could read my mind. That was it. I was gone. Totally gone. Nothing existed but him. His tongue. His chest pressed to my breasts. His lips demanding admission to my mouth. He devoured me, and I allowed it.

Wanted more.

He pulled away, and it took me several moments to remember where I was.

Shit. I had to stop acting like such a sex-crazed fool.

We were here on this new transport station... together. Not together.

Isaak was not my mate. He was not going back to Trion with me. I was not keeping him.

Pulling away, I moved toward the doors. "Let's go."

Strong hands pulled me back and settled me behind him. He was too damn tall, I couldn't see over his back. "Stay behind me, *gara*. I will protect you. This station is supposed to be a neutral meeting place, but if Cerberus' legion is here, they are not known to behave well."

My female pride was dinged, but I didn't argue. I bit my tongue because I was scared and nervous and in fucking outer space. And I would admit none of that.

Never appear weak. First lesson when growing up on the street. Never.

Isaak led me inside the bar, and I stayed close, following on his heels to a small table against one of the far walls with four chairs placed around it. In moments, he had entered our order into a screen on the tabletop and another robotic table on wheels had pulled up next to us. Isaak settled a dark red beverage in front of me and another for himself.

"What is it?" I asked.

"It's nutrient rich and tastes like sweet Atlan wine. It will nourish us and allow us to remain alert."

"Good idea." Drowning my nerves and the horror of that last couple days in alcohol was tempting, but I had thought long and hard about my life. I'd fight to death before I'd allow the blue lady, the slimy lizard man, or anyone else take me again. I'd left Earth to escape a shithole life. I'd be damned if I was going to settle for one out here.

Now, we had drinks before us, and another couple moved in close and sat down on the other side of the table. The alien—I assumed he was an alien by the sheer size of him and the dark green band on his arm—stood until the woman had taken her seat. Once she settled, he pulled his chair back and positioned it, so he could watch almost the entire room at once.

Isaak lifted his glass. "Zara, this is Ivy and Zenos."

Ivy smiled at me, and I about burst into tears. Shit. "Hi. You're from Earth?"

"Yes."

"Me too. Few years in the military on Earth. Then I volunteered to fight out here. Got assigned to a ReCon unit."

"You fought with them?" I motioned to the various sized giant aliens moving around the canteen.

Her grin turned into a laugh. "Yes. For a while. Then I lost my entire unit to a bad drug deal. I got out, got a bounty hunter's license from Prillon Prime, met Isaak here—" She pointed at the fidgeting male seated next to me. "Got some Hive tech, so I could fight the good fight and met Zenos on my way to Rogue 5."

"Hive tech?"

She wiggled her eyebrows. "Big business out here on the fringes. Anything you want. Bionic eyes. Arms. Legs. Hearing. I look human, but I'm not anymore. Not really."

I was not going to ask. "They let women fight in the Coalition?" I could totally see her wearing the black and gray armor, toting a space gun. She looked like a female Viking. Her long blonde hair was pulled back into a braid down her back. She was anything but dainty. Where she was fair, Zenos was dark. He looked... ruthless, but when his gaze was upon his mate, as it was now, it was surprisingly tender.

She shrugged. "It's a planet by planet rule. Most of the Coalition worlds want their women safe at home. But Earth girls are tougher than we look."

That made me smile. "Yes, we are."

"Besides, all these alien hotties are huge, but they're really just big teddy bears."

Zenos, who was twice the size of the largest human I'd ever met grumbled, and his skin actually turned hot pink. "I am not a bear. I tell you this, mate, repeatedly."

Her hand moved to rest on his thigh with a familiarity I envied. "And I've told you, repeatedly, that I can take care of myself." She gestured to the patrons lurking in dark spaces around the canteen. "Not one of these guys could take me."

He leaned in close. "Not one will get close enough to try."

She smiled at him, and I swear he melted. He had to be one of the Forsians Isaak had told me about. He was massive. And he melted. Doe eyes full of adoration for Ivy. Love. Clear as day.

Turning to me, she shrugged. "See? Teddy bears. Big ones." That fast, she was my new best friend. God, I had no idea how much seeing a familiar face—and human qualified as familiar out here—would affect me.

I really liked Ivy and her teddy bear mate, but this wasn't a local pub on a Friday night. And we weren't on a double date. While Isaak was the most intense and impressive lover I'd ever had—not that the list was long —he wasn't the dating type. Hell, all we'd done since we'd met besides the bout of sweaty, bossy sex had been to stay alive.

Didn't seem that Isaak was a date kind of guy. I never fell for romance and flowers myself.

Isaak spoke, finally. "You are much taller than Zara. Do females not have a standard size on Earth?"

I choked on my nutrient drink. Seriously? The first thing out of his mouth is comparing me—me, an average height, average everything—to a tall, willowy Nordic goddess?

Ivy raised her eyebrows. "I ate my veggies." She had to be close to six feet tall, and the guy she was with nearly two feet more. She leaned forward and rested her forearms on the table. "So, Zara from Boston, in his comm call, Isaak said you were an Interstellar Bride. He forgot to mention that you are his." Her pale eyes shifted to Isaak then back to me.

"I'm not Isaak's mate. My matched mate was murdered as soon as I transported to Trion."

Silence stretched, and I wondered if Ivy was in shock.

A group of rowdy males in Coalition uniform came into the place, went to the bar and ordered drinks. Isaak cleared his throat.

"I helped her escape Jirghogis on Omega Dome. He was supposed to hand her over to Cerberus. Ulza herself was there to take Zara back to Rogue 5." Isaak rubbed a hand over the back of his neck. "Ivy, you know I don't qualify to be tested. And no bride would want my ship as her home."

"Gwen likes a spaceship for a home just fine," Ivy replied. She looked to me to elaborate. "Gwen's human like you and me. She got matched to The Colony, and now she and her mate, Mak, roam the galaxy. Fighting evil and all that shit."

"Space pirates?" I asked, and Ivy laughed.

"More badass."

Isaak frowned. "What is this space pirate reference you keep saying?"

"On Earth, living in space is just a fantasy, even though we know of the Hive and the Coalition," Ivy explained to the guys. "It's not... real. Space pirates roam the galaxy to steal from the rich to give to the poor. They're infamous. Ruthless. Cunning. They kill bad guys and upset kingdoms. And do it all from a spaceship."

Isaak's hand settled on my thigh beneath the table. The heat from it warmed me in all kinds of places. "You think I am cunning and ruthless?"

I rolled my eyes when his chest puffed up with pride. "I'll admit, you've got skills."

He leaned in, and his breath fanned my ear. "At many things."

My pussy clenched remembering some of these things.

Weird music came from somewhere. Laughter came from a table behind me. No one was paying us any attention. For once.

"You are in trouble if Cerberus hunts you," Zenos said, bringing the conversation full circle. He crossed his arms over his massive chest. He wore the same black clothing as the bad guys at the Omega Dome, even down to the arm band, except his was a dark green instead of red. "Good thing we were close."

I shrugged, not sure what they were doing around here. I doubted errands. "I've had some problems," I said, simplifying the clusterfuck of my current situation.

Isaak laughed. "Problems? Trouble follows her. We even had a Spectra Five ship, tagged as from Cerberus, attack us more than fourteen hours out from Omega Dome."

I wasn't sure if I should be annoyed by his comment about trouble following me or admit he spoke the truth.

"Human females and trouble go hand in hand,"

Zenos intoned like a wise old sage.

"Hey!" Ivy countered, grinning. I had to assume she gave Zenos a run for his money.

"Who delivered you to Jirghogis?" Zenos asked.

All humor slipped from Isaak's face. "Bertok. A Councilor from Trion. He waited for Zara to transport from Earth, murdered her mate in front of her, chained her up, and when she woke up, she was on Omega Dome. What we can't figure out is why."

I was thankful he gave them the rundown of what had happened to me, so I didn't have to. I'd told him everything after the space attack, everything I knew. Everything I could remember or speculate. Both Ivy and Zenos remained quiet the entire time Isaak gave them a complete—well not complete—rundown of the last couple days. Ivy's pale brows winged up a few times, and Zenos' jaw clenched tight.

"Your mate was killed. This Trion Councilor Bertok brought you to Omega Dome?" Ivy asked.

I nodded. "To a slimy guy that smelled like swamp gas."

Ivy cringed. "I've heard about that guy, believe me. He's bad news, but there's worse out here. You have to be careful."

"Rumors from Rogue 5 are that Cerberus himself wants an Interstellar Bride," Zenos said. "And the only way he could get one would be to steal the female. He is not worthy."

Ivy agreed. "I guess we should have tried harder to kill him. Maybe we'll have to take it up with Astra next time we go back to Rogue 5."

"You live on Rogue 5?" I asked, trying to keep the

disgust out of my voice. I knew Zenos had on the arm band, but still, I hadn't made the connection.

Ivy shifted in her seat and took my hand across the table. "Rogue 5 is broken into multiple legions. They are all run like small kingdoms. Cerberus and Siren **CONFIRM** are vile. The rest do what they have to do to survive out here, but they aren't evil. We're with Astra legion. Mak, Gwen's mate, was part of Kronos legion. There's another human woman out here mated to the leader of Styx legion. And Cerberus hates Styx. I can see him wanting a human mate just because Styx has one. The asshole. God forbid you ended up in his bed."

I didn't even want to know...

"That explains Ulza's interest," Isaak added.

"Just confirming. Ulza is the blue lady, right?"

Isaak nodded. "She must have been the delivery person," he continued. "Cerberus wouldn't leave the moon base no matter how much he wants Zara. He would be too exposed."

Ivy and Zenos looked at each other.

"What?"

Ivy looked to me, licked her lips. "I've had a run in with Cerberus myself."

"You dealt with this guy?" I asked.

She gave a slight shrug. "It's a long story, but Cerberus hates my guts."

Zenos focused his attention on me, and all traces of teddy bear were gone. Like, scary gone. "Since Cerberus legion was after you, the rumor must be true. It would make sense he wants an Earth female like you and Ivy—" He looked to his mate. "—for his own." Zenos pulled Ivy in for a swift, fierce kiss.

I flicked my gaze at Isaak, but he didn't seem surprised. Nor did he appear inclined to kiss me. Darn it. Not that I wanted Isaak to claim me like that. Right? In front of the whole canteen? Like I was his? Zenos was definitely claiming Ivy in front of everyone, and if Cerberus were here, he'd know exactly who Ivy belonged to. And who he would have to kill to get to her.

Ivy had to be one of the safest females in the universe. I envied the hell out of her. I didn't know what it felt like to be safe. Not on Earth. Not out here in space. I'd felt safe for all of five minutes when I was with Isaak, but then we'd been attacked, and the illusion I'd been allowing myself had shattered into a million pieces. I wasn't safe. I would never be safe.

Better make peace with that shit and stop wanting to cry like a baby. "Okay, so Cerberus has a hard-on for an Earth girl. Why didn't Bertok deliver me directly to him?" I wondered.

When Zenos looked my way, his gaze was full of defiant rage but not directed at me. "No outsider goes to Rogue 5 alone. Not if they want to survive the trip. We make sure of it."

Ivy laughed. "Trust me on that one. We go home, get inside Astra territory, and we are snug as a bug in a rug."

I nodded, totally envious.

"If Bertok knew of Cerberus' interest and heard about you being matched," Zenos mused. "Maybe he killed your mate, so he could sell you to Cerberus. He would have had to use an intermediary. Bertok couldn't get to Rogue 5. Not only is it impossible to get past our defense system, but Trion is at the far end of the galaxy. Transport only. No ship can make that trip. Means he had to meet Cerberus somewhere in the middle."

"The dome and Jirghogis," Isaak said, frowning. "Ulza's from Cerberus. She was at Omega Dome for business with me. Cerberus must have sent her to escort you back to Rogue 5's moon base."

"Still peddling Hive tech?" Ivy asked.

Isaak tipped his head. "Sure am. How're the parts?"

Zenos growled. "Her parts are fine."

I frowned, looked at Ivy. She had Hive parts. She'd mentioned that a few minutes ago? Didn't look like it, unless they made her into a giant. Her eyes looked normal. Maybe she had cyborg hearing or something. Would it be rude to ask?

Yes. Yes, it would be rude.

"So, I got away. Yay!" I said, full of sarcasm and getting back on track. "But they still want me? They came after us. Why me? Can't Cerberus just get another human somewhere else?"

It made no sense although I was thrilled that I wasn't Cerberus' new mate. Based on the way Zenos' face frowned when he spoke of the guy, I felt like I lucked out.

Zenos nodded. "Yes, their continued pursuit shows you are important."

"I'm not that exciting."

The three of them stared at me.

"*Fark.*" Isaak looked away, thought for a moment. "I've been stupid. My ship has stealth technology. Hive tech. Best there is," Isaak shared. "It can't be followed."

Ivy sat back in her chair, crossed her arms then nodded in my direction. "So, if they can't track your ship, they must have been tracking her."

I pointed at myself. "Me?"

"There's no other way they'd have known where we were," Isaak clarified.

Lifting my hand, I tapped my fingers against my temple. "They gave me an NPU back at the Brides Testing center. You have one," I said to Ivy. "Could that track me with that?"

She shook her head. "Prillon Prime could do it, track your location I mean, but the tech is tightly controlled. If Cerberus had it, we all would have heard about it by now. At least within Astra legion. He would be wreaking havoc all over the place."

"She has typical Trion adornments, but I've inspected those thoroughly." Isaak's words had my cheeks heating. I smacked him on the shoulder. Hard. He looked to me, eyes wide and rubbed his arm as Ivy and Zenos grinned. "What?"

"Are all space men this obtuse?" I asked, looking to Ivy. She might be from Earth, but she'd been in space for a lot longer than I.

Ivy made a sound between a huff and a snort. "Yes. And possessive."

Isaak held up a hand in surrender. "All I'm saying is, I've checked every inch of you. All that's on you are the Trion adornments and your Earth belly button bar and necklace."

I frowned, tugged the loose choker Bertok had put up on me from beneath my top. "This? It's not mine."

Zenos sat forward so fast I didn't get a chance to blink before he stared at it. "That's not from Earth," he repeated. "That's from Rogue 5."

I tried to look down at the necklace, but it only made my eyes hurt. "Rogue 5?"

"*Fark*," Isaak hissed. "I thought it was something from Earth, something personal. We need to get that off her. Now."

Zenos stood, came around the table and batted my hand away. "Allow me, please."

"I have never seen a necklace like that," Ivy said. She stood behind her mate, watching.

Zenos' fingers brushed against my neck and collarbones. "It's locked."

"May I try?" Isaak asked.

Zenos looked at Isaak over my shoulder then let go of the necklace and moved away.

"*Gara*, turn toward me."

I spun around in the chair eager to have it off. Knowing it wasn't supposed to be there, that it was not a typical Trion adornment, made me feel as if a snake were wrapped around my neck. He pulled some weird tool from his belt, held it up. "This won't hurt. Much."

My eyes widened. "Much?"

He grinned then winked. I exhaled.

"Those are hard to come by," Ivy said, her voice sounding impressed. "Looks like you hit the jackpot in Hive tech."

As Isaak worked on removing the necklace, I stayed still, noticed the color of his eyes, the sharpness of his jaw. Those full lips. "Hard to come by? For you, maybe." Those full lips moved, and I watched as the corner tipped up.

"That's right, Space Pirate," Ivy countered. "You can get anything."

With an audible click, the necklace loosened. Isaak looked up and winked at me, slid the metal from my skin and handed it to Zenos, who'd settled back across the table.

Zenos looked at it closely, Ivy's head moving beside his to stare as well. "This is Tryphite. It's only found in one mine on Rogue 5's home planet, Hyperion. You can tell by the silver sheen but the tinge of green. It's heavy, yet pliable. It can't be forged with any other metal, no matter the melting point. It's like the stuff has a mind of its own." He spoke like a scientist who knew his stuff.

"Why did Bertok have it?" I wondered.

Zenos flicked his gaze to me. "I do not know, but it proves the connection between Bertok and Rogue 5."

Ivy reached for the medallion and ran her fingernail along the edges. "It looks like a locket. There must be something inside."

Zenos grunted. "Only one way to find out." He walked to the bar top until he came to the very end. There, sitting alone and looking angry, was a single male wearing a wine-red arm band.

"Oh, shit." Ivy shot to her feet.

"What's going on?" I asked.

When I made a move to step around the table, Isaak's arm wrapped around my waist from behind and held me back. I hadn't even noticed that he stood. "Leave him, *gara*. It's too dangerous."

I wanted to argue, I really did, but he was warm and strong, and Ivy had stopped moving too, her hands on her hips like an annoyed wife.

Zenos walked to the male who looked up from his

drink. Zenos said something I could not hear, lifted his fist and swung. Hard.

The Cerberus male, who had lines on his face and a thin, sunken face, flew back into the wall and slumped there unconscious.

"What the hell is he doing?" I asked.

Ivy turned to me, shrugged and turned back to watch Zenos bend down, wipe something from the male's mouth and return to the table.

"Give me the medallion."

Ivy handed it over without question.

Zenos lifted his thumb, and I saw a drop of blood on the tip. He rubbed the liquid on the surface of the medallion and set it back down on the table. "Cerberus codes all of his tech to artificial DNA that every member of his legion is required to carry."

"What?"

Ivy scowled as she watched the medallion. "It's crazy out here, Zara. And even worse on Rogue 5. Don't ask."

I didn't want to, and even if I did, I doubted I would understand her answer. I had to work two jobs just to eat. I barely finished high school. DNA sounded like science to me, and that was so not my territory.

A pale light appeared along the edges of the medallion, and as one, we all four sank back down into our chairs to watch as the medallion opened up, the top sliding back and away into the sides like a collapsing accordion with metallic ridges.

Inside was a small clear crystal.

"What is that?" I asked.

Ivy reached for it, and Zenos waited, her much

smaller fingers lifting the pea size crystal from a lined bed of some kind. "Data."

Isaak frowned. "What's on it? What could Bertok possibly send to Cerberus?"

Zenos crossed his arms and all traces of the teddy bear were long gone. In the corner, the Cerberus male had begun to move his legs. He was coming around, and I really didn't want to be here when he woke up. "Can we go? That Cerberus guy is moving."

Isaak rested a hand on my shoulder. "No one will harm you, *gara*. You have my word."

Ivy glanced back over her shoulder, watched the moaning, groaning alien try to roll over, and turned back to face me. "Zara is right. We should get out of here. Even if he didn't already alert Cerberus to your presence here, he will now."

Zenos agreed. "We will take this data crystal back to Rogue 5 and find out what information it contains."

Ivy looked at Isaak. "What about you? They'll have every bounty hunter and scavenger out here looking for you. It won't be safe. Won't matter where you go."

Isaak looked at me, our gazes locking and the look in his eyes dark. Intense. Impossible to read. "Zara and I will transport to my home on Trion. Bertok will not be expecting us. Zara has only been away from his side for two days. On Trion, that will be less than an hour. He will not even be looking. We will go to my home and wait to hear from you. Zara will be safe there."

"Uhm-hmmm." Ivy made the odd noise, and I tore my gaze from Isaak to look at her. She winked at me. "Not yours, Isaak. You sure about that?"

"Ivy!" I protested. No, Isaak was not mine. And he didn't want to be mine. End of story.

She lifted her hands, stepped forward and gave me a hug. I squeezed back. Hard. "Welcome to space, Zara."

"Thanks."

She took Zenos' hand like they were young lovers out for a Sunday stroll, walked out of the canteen while the Cerberus male was still incoherent. Isaak's hand was in mine seconds later. "Let's go, Zara. It's time for me to go home."

saak

IT HAD BEEN four years since I'd been in this house. Mansion. Four years for me but just over one month for my family. Too soon to expect anything to have changed. The thick marble of the place still gleamed like a beacon. Built to withstand the blistering desert sun and constant heat, it was built with thick stone quarried from the region's vast mines. It held in the coolness while large windows in every room offered views. While I liked things simple and kept furnishings to a minimum, it lacked for nothing. Just like any household that was part of High Councilor Henrick's family. While nothing had changed, not a piece of furniture moved, it looked different. *I* was different. I'd had a staff, a full contingency of servants befitting a rich son of a High Councilor, but when I'd left, I'd paid them handsomely and relocated them to work a cousin's estate. Since there wasn't a layer of dust on every surface, it seemed someone had defied my orders and remained behind. Perhaps it was my mother's doing, maintaining a constant vigil that I might someday return.

Well, that time had come. All because of the female beside me.

While that was true, it was also because of Bertok. He was up to something. Something bad. So bad that he'd murdered an innocent man for his bride, sold her to a known trader in the outer reaches to pass on to the leader of the most ruthless legion on Rogue 5. He'd received credit for Zara, but there was more. He could have earned that from selling her to anyone. No, Bertok and Cerberus had made a deal, and it all had to do with that necklace I'd ridiculously thought was a human decoration, just like her navel ring.

While I'd left so long ago, I was still bitter. Still angry at my family. Yet Trion was my home, and I couldn't let Bertok live knowing what he'd done to Zara. What he intended to do with Cerberus. I didn't need to have the details of their plan to assume it was very, very bad. Cerberus' depths of evil had yet to be plumbed... and I knew more stories than most because of Zenos and Ivy.

Based on Zenos' drive to learn the truth about the other legion's leader, he, too, was rightfully concerned.

I dropped my bag on the tile floor by the entry, looked to Zara. I was exhausted. I didn't transport often, preferring to travel by my ship. That wasn't possible coming to Trion, and I'd forgotten how it sucked the energy from my body.

We'd come from Zenith directly here. It wasn't the

time for sightseeing. The transport center was large, and I hoped my return was not noticed by anyone familiar to me. I would have to visit my parents eventually, but by the way Zara was swaying on her feet, I didn't want it to happen right away. I wasn't ready to deal with them on top of everything else.

I wondered how she saw the place. It was vast. Elegant. Larger than any bachelor could ever want or need. *Fark*, even larger than any Trion family could ever use. This being my home, it was representative of me or at least of the life I'd left behind. I didn't usually care what others thought of me. Hell, I'd left the planet for just such a reason. I cared what Zara thought, though.

"You're rich," she said finally.

"My family is," I replied, clarifying the difference.

"If you have all this, why are you selling Hive tech for your cannon thing? Just write a check or something."

I sighed. Zara had said she'd grown up poor, and I was sure such opulence was new to her, just as much as being on a new planet.

"It's family money that built this place. Not mine. My parents' home is larger still. My dead brother, Malik's, equally so. I haven't touched a credit of it since I left. Come on, let's get some rest." I took her elbow to guide her toward the stairs and the second floor that housed the seven bedrooms.

She shrugged out of my hold. "We're on Trion. We need to find Bertok."

I couldn't help but smile. "*Gara,* I'm exhausted. I'm not sure how you're still standing. You've barely slept since you came from Earth and have transported three times. An Atlan beast would be struggling to stay conscious. Leave your titan stick by the door, and we'll sleep."

"I have motivation," she replied, her jaw clenched, her pale eyes fierce as she looked up at me.

"Remember we talked about the way time is different on Trion? The planet is so distant in the sector that it's been—" I paused and did some loose math in my head. "—about two hours here on Trion since Bertok returned from The Dome."

Her mouth fell open. "Two hours?"

It had been three days since we'd been beneath The Dome, so it was hard to even fathom the bend in time. It was even harder to fathom how my life had changed since then.

"Bertok is not expecting us, and I'm sure he's sleeping off his own transport. While it would be a good time to attack, we don't know all the details. Yet. There's nothing for us to do now but rest and wait for Zenos and Ivy to investigate. Remember, while we sleep, days will pass for them."

Her shoulders slumped. "Daylight savings time is one thing, but this? I don't think I'll ever understand this... time change." She rubbed her eyes. "Rest sounds good. A shower sounds better."

Nodding, I led her into my bed chamber and through to the bathing room. Everything was as pristine as when I'd left it. The deep stone tub, the windows that surrounded it to make the user feel decadent soaking in a pool of water surrounded by the barrenness of the desert landscape. While we were close to the city, wealth afforded untarnished views. I didn't remember the room to be so large although anything was expansive after the tiniest of bathing rooms on my ship.

It was this... this excess that I'd abandoned. But now I was back.

With a human. No, with a Trion bride.

Even though I'd seen every inch of Zara, I retreated, allowing her some privacy.

"Um, I have no idea how to use that." She pointed at the shower tube when I turned back to face her. "And the tub is like a swimming pool. I'm so tired I might drown."

She was small and fierce, but I continued to forget she had yet to settle anywhere in space. She'd moved from Trion to The Dome to Transport Station Zenith and then back to Trion. The entire time, she'd been in danger. She still was, until we heard otherwise from Zenos.

I took my time and showed her how the bathing tube worked, steam immediately beginning to fill the room. I pointed out the other features she might need then left. It was my job to see to her needs were met, even the most basic ones.

I used a second bathing room—*fark*, I had enough of them—to wash the travels from my own body. I thought of Zara naked and wet, using my scented soap over her pale skin. My cock stirred to life, it seemed a constant thing whenever I thought of the female. She'd responded so beautifully, albeit prickly, to my commands on the ship. I'd begun to master her body. Her mind was another challenge entirely. One I ultimately planned to win. She just didn't know it yet.

By the time I returned to my chamber, naked and beyond exhausted, Zara was in my bed, asleep. I climbed in behind her and tugged her close. Pulling the fresh sheets up and over us, I called out. "Blinds close."

Yes, someone had been maintaining the property, for the house responded by immediately completing my simple command. The room quickly darkened, and I slept, knowing this peace was short lived. Bertok had to be dealt with—Cerberus was Zenos' problem—and then there were my parents. I could handle ion fire and even rogue asteroids, but I wasn't sure I could survive seeing the pain in my mother's eyes.

———

I AWOKE to Zara's face looming over me. Sleeping deeply, I hadn't felt her shift in my arms or rise up to her elbow. I blinked, took in her refreshed face, the curious gaze, even in the dim lighting. I had no idea what time it was or how long we'd slept, but I felt better. Perhaps it was the naked body pressed against mine. My cock certainly rose because of that.

"Blinds open," I called.

Zara looked about as the room brightened, the strong Trion sun cutting through the room's windows.

"Being rich has its perks," she murmured.

"You are fixated upon wealth," I replied drily.

"Says the guy who's got voice activated curtains." She pushed her hair back.

It had been wet when she'd fallen asleep, and now it was a wild tangle. I itched to touch the wild strands, so I did.

"I told you I grew up poor. My entire apartment could fit in that bathtub of yours."

"This house is part of my family's wealth. Not mine. I haven't earned it."

"You were born into it. What's wrong with that? It's not like you stole it from people."

I frowned then shook my head. "No, my family is not bad."

"Then why walk away from them? I mean, you said you were gone four years. That's a long time."

My family dynamics weren't simple. Even if I explained everything to Zara, she still might not understand, just as my parents still didn't. We were from different planets, different cultures, even if she'd been matched to Trion. She found my wealth interesting. No, she found how I turned my back on it intriguing. Perhaps even insulting, to have access to such lavish things and not take advantage. And for reasons I could not explain, I needed her to understand.

"Remember, it was four years for me, but it's only been about a month to them." I sighed. "I did not come into this world alone. I had a twin brother. Malik. He was born first and became my father's heir."

I paused, expecting Zara to interrupt with questions, but for once, she remained silent. Patient. Waited for me to find the words I needed.

"Malik was beautiful. He had our mother's dark skin and wild curls. He laughed at everything. He loved people. Everyone. He could sit for hours studying history or reading ancient texts. He had our law books memorized by age fifteen and Coalition Fleet regulations at seventeen. He understood politics, alliances, knew how to read people. He always seemed to know what to say to gain their trust."

Zara's hand slid up onto my chest to rest over my heart, and I wrapped my hand around hers, taking the small comfort as memories of my brother bubbled up like a raw wound, and the pain I'd spent the past four years running from exploded within me like a desert storm, the grains of sand rubbing me raw from the inside out.

"You loved him," she said. "A lot."

"Yes. Everyone in the region loved him. He had two dozen mating offers by the time we were twelve."

She lifted her pale gaze to mine, whispered, "So what happened?"

"I did. I find history, politics and law to be an absolute bore. I could not sit still for lessons and constantly found myself in trouble. As often as my father praised Malik, he took me to task." I paused, remembering one instance that buried the pain and made me laugh. "When we were eleven, I convinced Malik that we needed to capture and tame our own wild mounts. So, we packed a pair of reins and snuck out under the double moons to stalk the hairy beasts."

"And?"

"And we found them, all right. Right next to a den of —well, you won't know what they are—but their defense is a pungent spray that soaks the skin and hair."

"Like a skunk?"

"I do not know a skunk, but one of the wild mounts kicked me because while they are big and fierce, they fear the smelly vermin. I flew into the nearby nest, and the smaller creatures sprayed me from head to toe."

"Oh, no." Her eyes were alight with laughter, and I knew she grasped the concept of the creatures at least.

"Malik had to practically carry me home since we were stupid enough to forget a ReGen wand. I had three broken ribs, a broken arm from the kick, and I reeked of this, as you say, skunk-like spray. We both had to bathe. We tried everything but could not get the scent from my hair. So Malik shaved my head then shaved his own to match. He sneaked down to the medic's office and brought a ReGen wand to heal my broken bones, and then we both lied to our parents, saying we saw the bald head of one of the guards and decided we liked the look."

Zara was chuckling now. "They believed you?"

The happiness died in my heart as the memory came to its inevitable conclusion. "They pretended to. But that night, when Malik was out with one of his tutors and I was alone, my father came to me, as he did many times, and berated me for being a bad influence on my brother. Because of me, Malik risked his life unnecessarily, stole from the doctor, lied to his parents, and looked like a fool with his head shaved."

She frowned. "That's terrible. You were just boys having fun. That's what kids do."

"Not when you are the son of a High Councilor."

"I'm sorry."

"I was angry. At myself. At my brother. Because my father was right. It happened over and over again. I was always getting Malik into trouble. The day he died, I had convinced him to steal a desert rover with me. We were out jumping sand dunes when he lost control and the vehicle flipped, crushing him. I had a ReGen wand this time, but it wasn't enough. He died before the medical teams could arrive."

"It was an accident, Isaak."

"It was no accident that I convinced Malik to go. He was supposed to be studying."

"How old were you?"

"Twenty. It was a week before our birthday."

She didn't speak, just wrapped her arms around me and rested her cheek over my heart. Her silence gave me the courage to finish.

"I was on my knees in the desert, crying over my brother's dead body when my parents arrived." I shuddered. I couldn't stop my body's reaction to the memory. "My father stood over me and told me the wrong son had died that day."

She gasped, her eyes wide. "Oh my God. No, Isaak. He didn't mean that! He was in pain."

"No, *gara*, he was right. Malik was better than I am, in every way."

"That's bullshit. Would he have fought Ulza for me? Would he have been able to hunt and kill Hive the way you do? How many lives have you saved? There's no way to know. Hundreds? Thousands? Sounds like your brother was charming and a bookworm, but there's more to life than history books. More to being a leader than making friends. Sometimes, you have to be ruthless to survive. Your brother needed you to be exactly the way you are." She squeezed me tightly, and the pain in my chest lessened.

"My father made it very clear that I was not wanted here, *gara*. I remained for some time but couldn't take it any longer. Fled the planet. If not for you, I would not have come back."

"Then I'm grateful for everything. You can't outrun pain, Isaak. And you shouldn't carry it around like a boulder, either. Malik made the choice to go with you, to drive the vehicle, to jump the sand dune. He was with you every step of the way. You two were probably inseparable."

"We were twins." That was all the explanation required.

"Exactly. Malik needed you to help him break free. Trust me on that." Zara's stomach rumbled loudly, breaking into our conversation as if there was some kind of wild animal in the room with us.

She blushed, as if that was the most scandalous thing about her body. Or, perhaps, because she did not want me to infer anything about *her needs* from her last comment.

While I wanted to remain abed and fuck her back into exhaustion, Zara required food. So did I for what I wished to do to her. I also didn't wish to speak further of my family troubles.

I pushed back the covers, climbed from the bed. "Come, I shall feed you." I went to a closet where I knew the customary Trion clothing I'd left behind was freshly laundered and orderly. I tugged on a pair of loose pants and was tying the string at the waist when Zara appeared in the doorway. Naked save for the rings in her nipples, the chain between them and the small bar in her navel.

My cock tented my pants, and Zara's eyes as she watched it happen didn't help. I growled, randomly grabbed a shirt and tossed it at her. "Your body is a taunt, *gara.* However, your hunger must be satiated first."

"You'll fuck me after I've been fed then?" she asked, her head lost beneath the fabric as she put it on. It hung loosely on her and almost to her knees, covering her with more modesty than most Trion dresses. The outline of her nipples, the rings and chain couldn't be missed.

Fark.

"Come," I said, leading her downstairs and to the kitchen. It was vast, with stone floors, large counter surfaces and the most technologically advanced cooking equipment.

She stood and stared. "I thought you only used that weird machine."

I went to the food storage, opened the door. Filled with prepared meals. I had to hope that whomever replenished it ate what would have otherwise spoiled. "That is in space. Here on Trion, there are kitchens. Food is cooked."

"By you or a chef?" she wondered.

I looked at her around the door frame. "A chef, of course. What rich person cooks?" I asked, my words so laced with sarcasm she couldn't miss it.

"Got it," she said, looking away. "I'll stop poking the bear."

I frowned, not sure what that meant. "There are many meal options to choose from. Shall I choose a variety for you to try?"

"Yes, please."

I took various items and placed them on the table then retrieved serving utensils and glasses of water to drink.

I directed her to sit then settled myself across from her.

She touched a container, pulled her hand back. "It's warm. I expected it to be chilled."

I tipped my head toward the food storage. "It is cold

within; however, the container begins to warm it once it is removed. I trust they will be all heated appropriately by now."

Taking off the lids of each, she peeked at the food, then tasted a little bit of each. I watched her as she ate, quickly learning the Trion foods she liked and the ones she truly enjoyed. I ate my favorite dish, one I hadn't had since I'd been on-planet last. We didn't speak other than when I pointed out what she was eating, how it was cooked, and the spices involved. When she was full, she set her cutlery down, wiped her mouth with a napkin.

"I think I'm going to like Trion food. Perhaps *that* was why I was matched to the planet." Her smile was bright and her eyes alive with teasing. She was fed and rested and... not her usual feisty self. Although this was the first time she was either fed or rested as well as not in danger.

"*That* is not the only reason. Trion culture satisfies your other cravings as well."

My cock stirred again at the idea of spreading her out across the table and tasting *her*. There was time. We had yet to hear from Zenos although with the way time bended between Trion and other places in the universe, I expected it anytime.

"What other cravings?"

So she chose to be coy. She had not been so reserved while riding my cock. "Your need to surrender, to feel safe. To let go. You hunger to be conquered, *gara*."

Zara blushed, bit her lip. "No. It wasn't like that. I'm not like that."

I arched a brow. "Really? Then it wasn't your pussy that dripped at my command?"

Her mouth opened, and she stared at me wide

eyed. As if while she was brutally honest and straightforward with many things, her sexuality was not one of them. I crooked my finger, beckoning her to me. She swallowed hard but stood and came around the table.

I turned and parted my knees, so she could stand between. "*Gara*—"

"Zara," she countered.

"No one has called you an endearment before? Is that why you are so against it?"

She pursed her lips. "An endearment means there is a connection, something special between two people. We don't have that."

I stifled a smile, for I knew she'd perhaps knee me in the balls for it. She was good at denying herself, at avoiding what was right in front of her. Me. Of this... chemistry we had.

"Zara, *gara,* you do not feel the connection?" I set my hands on her thighs, slid the soft fabric of the shirt she wore--my shirt--up. Higher and higher.

She didn't move. *Fark,* she didn't even breathe. She could step back at any time, but she didn't. My touch was something she wanted, the anticipation of what I'd do next was something she craved.

The air was still, the sun warm through the windows. The house was silent except for our breathing. No one was chasing us. No one was shooting at us. No one needed us. We were free to explore what this was between us.

I cupped her pussy, felt her desire. Her heat. She startled but didn't move away. Her eyes flared. "Do you know what the nipple rings and chain are for?" I asked.

She shook her head but held herself still. I didn't do more than pet her pussy. Slowly. Gently.

"They are for your mate to affix his medallion, so everyone knows who serves and protects her."

"That's sexist as hell."

I offered a slight shrug. "It is the male who is kept, who is permanently chained to his mate."

"I'm not your mate," she snapped.

"You may not belong to me, but your pussy does."

She tried to step back, but I curled a finger into her. Her inner walls clenched down upon it.

"Whose hand is coated in your need?"

I pressed against her G-spot, waited.

"Yours," she said finally.

Pulling my hand from her, I set her back a step, so I could stand. I went to the S-Gen machine in the kitchen, but I didn't order up food. In moments, I opened the door and returned to my seat before her. I held up the item. Two golden spheres attached by a small chain that ran between them, and another, much longer chain with a marked golden disc attached to its terminal end.

She stared at it.

"It is time to show you the pleasure of a Trion female. Shirt off, please."

I didn't explain what the spheres were for. She'd find out soon enough. Her curiosity got the better of her, for she lifted my shirt off and dropped it to the floor.

"Ah, so beautiful," I praised. "Feet wider apart."

When she complied, I held onto a single gold ball and let the second, along with the chain, dangle.

"Um, what are you doing?" she asked when I carefully nudged the sphere up and into her pussy. It was an easy task with how wet she was. "I'm not much for weird sex toys."

I didn't say anything as I set the second sphere inside her.

Removing my hand, she gasped, and her hips curled back, a sign she was clenching hard to hold the objects within. The chain dangled down between her parted thighs, the medallion at the bottom offering some weight.

I watched her closely. Arousal, frustration, anger, surprise, so many emotions flitted across her face. "Isaak," she breathed.

"You have your safe word, *gara*. Do you wish to use it?"

She hadn't said no yet, a sign in itself she wasn't rejecting my attentions. I wanted to remind her though that I would stop at any time. I needed to know her limits. I instinctively had an idea of what they were, but Zara was unlike any female I'd ever met. While she tested to Trion, she wasn't actually from the planet. I didn't know how deep her needs ran, but I was quickly learning.

"No," she said finally.

"Don't let the spheres fall out. Trion females are punished for such an infraction."

Her head whipped up to look at me. "Punished? God, Isaak, it's going to make me come."

"I haven't even turned it on yet."

Her eyes widened to the size of dinner plates. "On?"

I pressed a button on the remote I hadn't allowed her to see, and her knees bent. She gasped, her hand smacking onto the table beside her. "Isaak! You're being an asshole."

"Ah, there's the Zara I know so well." Instantly, I turned it off.

"The neuroprocessor within will take you to the brink of orgasm, then retreat, never allowing you satisfaction."

She glanced up at me, her cheeks flushed. "What's the fun in that?"

"There is none. The female has her focus squarely on her pussy and not whatever wrongdoing she has been caught in. Those who see the medallion and chain know she has been... naughty."

Her head swung left and right? "Who's going to see?"

"Claimings are public. A woman's arousal and pleasure are to be shared and shown off."

"Share and show me off and not only will I say my safeword, but your balls will be lodged so far up in your throat, you'll be choking on them."

Instantly, I turned off the vibrations.

"No!" she cried.

That was not what I expected to hear.

"You wish the device to remain on?"

She launched herself at me, the medallion at the end of the chain smacking me in the leg. I grabbed her and held her in my arms as she kissed me. Fiercely, wildly. I kissed her back. Devoured her. Turning, I reached out and swiped my hand across the dining table, clearing it of everything from our meal. I leaned forward, resting Zara upon the hard surface. Our faces were inches apart, her breath fanning my cheek.

"It's not yours to control, is it? That's what you like." I understood. The stimspheres provided a different kind of lesson for Zara, that her pleasure, the look on her face of pure bliss, was mine to give her. Her eyes were

133

closed, her lips swollen and parted. Her cheeks were flushed. "I will not share you, *gara*. Not ever. Your orgasms, your cries of pleasure, your sighs. The look of you now spread out before me is just for me. No one else."

She arched her back and set her feet on the edge of the table. So uninhibited, lost to the power of the stimspheres. "You'll not come from this. They are programmed to never allow a female to climax."

"Isaak," she whimpered, clearly wanting just that.

Tugging on the chain, I plucked the spheres from her, one at a time. The wet sound of her arousal indicating how much satisfaction her body found in them.

"You'll only come from my fingers, my mouth, my cock."

I gave her the first, slipping two fingers inside her. Yes, she was dripping with her need. Dropping to my knees on the floor, I pushed her thighs wide, tugged her hips to the edge of the table and devoured her, as if I hadn't just had a meal. She was my succor, my survival.

I was drowning in her. The silky feel of her. The heat. Her scent. Her flavor. It was all as wild as she was. I could have continued to taunt her, to flick the little pearl until she was ripping out my hair and begging, but I wanted to witness her pleasure once more.

Slipping two fingers inside her once again, I worked her with those digits as my tongue laved her, licked her. I sucked and tugged, worked her clit until her thighs clamped over my ears, and she creamed my mouth.

Fark, was she perfect. Uninhibited.

Slowly, I stood, shucked my clothes, set my hand by her head and leaned over her as I worked my cock into her. She was sweaty and replete, lost to her pleasure. To what I gave her.

"Isaak," she moaned, and she clenched down on me hard.

I held still. Waited, which was torture.

Her eyes blinked open, and I watched as they cleared of her desire enough to see me.

"There you are. Ready to get fucked?"

She lifted a hand and cupped my jaw. "I can't say you're a selfish lover." Her voice was a mix of breathy desire and grumbling.

"You may submit, *gara,* but you will always come first. Always."

The glazed look of desire in her eyes threatened my control. "Hands to your knees. Open yourself to me."

She did as I asked, her hands pulling her legs up and back, exposing her pussy. Opening her up like a flower.

"More. Tilt your hips. I want everything."

"Isaak."

She said my name, not *master,* but I did not have the heart to deny myself, not when I knew our time together could come to an abrupt end.

I'd had enough talking. I pulled back, thrust deep. Took her hard. Took her as I needed it to know she was right here with me. Beneath me. Mine.

Her pleasure milked me hard, and I wasn't strong enough to resist.

The orgasm built at the base of my spine, zapped the energy from my body and thrust it deep into Zara along with my seed. Setting my forehead against hers, I breathed in her air, her life force just as I gave her mine deep into her pussy.

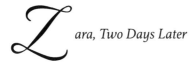

ara, Two Days Later

NOTHING COULD HAVE PREPARED me for life on Trion. At every meal, each bite was an explosion of taste and textures on my tongue. Sweet. Salty. Bitter. Rich. The food overwhelmed my taste buds the way the clothing seduced my skin. Except for the first night of our arrival, when I'd worn Isaak's shirt, he'd made traditional Trion outfits out of the cool clothing-making machine. I didn't know what the sheer, gossamer fabrics were made of, but they were softer than silk, light as air, and clung to every curve with constant caressing every bare part of me. I wore no underwear, no bra. I was beginning to feel like I wore nothing but nipple rings, chain between and air, the experience shockingly sexy.

I *felt* sexy. Beautiful. Adored. Me. I felt *feminine.*

Isaak constantly touched me, kissed me, fucked me

until my eyes rolled back into my head, and I was lost to the pleasure. Guilt tore at me, thoughts of Naron, my dead mate, the guy perfectly matched to me by the Brides' Program, made me wonder if I was living some kind of mistake with Isaak. He wasn't meant to be mine nor I his. He wasn't my perfect match. I hadn't come all the way to space to be his. He wasn't the Trion male the Interstellar Brides' processing center had matched to me, and I felt... bad for being... happy with him. In so many ways.

Why did I want him so badly? Why did I miss his touch on my skin the moment he left my side? Why did my heart jump every time I saw him?

Why did I love the way he called me *gara*? Why did I submit to him so easily? I wasn't that kind of woman. Never had been. I was a fighter. A scrapper. A girl from the neighborhood who had grown up tough.

This soft, submissive female was not me. This silk and gold and hair flowing free and loose down my back was not me.

More importantly—more of a confusion than any other thought swirling in my head—if he wasn't supposed to be mine, why was I falling in love? That completely freaked me out. How could I be feeling this way for him? He was *so* annoying. So frustrating. I wanted to strangle him and kiss the life out of him. I didn't trust men let alone love them.

Feet bare, I curled my toes into one of the deepest, softest rugs I'd ever walked upon and ran my hand over the edge of a statue of a beast that looked like a cross between a horse and a bear.

"Sure feels like me," I muttered to myself.

"What are you worrying about, *gara?* I recognize the look in your eyes." Isaak appeared in the large room as if from nowhere and wrapped his arms around me. The heavy weight of his armor pressed into my body through my thin gown, and I gasped as the rough edges made contact with the sensitive flesh of my bottom. Isaak had spent a good amount of time making my backside burn last night. Spanking me because I still would not call him master.

I couldn't. I knew if I did, I'd be lost. Totally screwed. In love. In too deep to save myself. Feeling this way was one thing, but admitting it aloud to myself and to Isaak was something else entirely.

If I called him master, I'd get hurt. I still didn't completely understand what had happened between Isaak and his parents, and I didn't think he was a criminal on Trion. But even so, not once had he said he wanted to stay.

No, he paced the house like a caged beast while I reveled in the cold stone walls under my hands, the soft desert breezes coming through the open windows. He'd told me about the time bend although it didn't seem real, but the two days we'd been on Trion had been much longer for Ivy and Zenos. It had been weeks for them. Weeks to work the Cerberus angle, yet we'd had no word from them. I was just glad for the break, for a moment to just... be. I wandered the enclosed gardens, listened to birdsong I'd never heard before, touched flower petals so soft I scarce believed they could be real, and never wanted to leave. Yeah, I was weird and sappy, but there was peace in this house. Peace. Power. Safety. All the things I'd left Earth to find.

Hot sex with Isaak wasn't going to be enough for me though. I didn't want to live in a tiny room in a spaceship. I was well aware that Isaak didn't want to live here. I wasn't an idiot. This thing between us was incredible, but it wasn't going to last. I wanted to be settled. He wanted to roam. To search the galaxy for... I had no idea what.

I'd done the same thing. Volunteered because I was searching for something more. Something not found at home. I now believed I had it here on Trion with Isaak. Was it him I wanted or this place? The answer came easily. It wasn't either or. It was both. I wanted to be here with him.

"*Gara.*" Isaak turned me in his arms until I faced him, my breasts crushed against the hard outline of his armor. The contrast made my pussy clench with heat.

"Yes?"

He blinked, startled. "No protest this time?"

I huffed out a little laugh. "No." I didn't have the heart, not when I knew this was like some kind of dream, and any moment Ivy and Zenos would call and force us both to wake up.

Two fingers under my chin, Isaak angled my head up until I gave in to his unspoken demand and looked him in the eye. "What are you thinking, Zara? I don't like what I see in your eyes."

I frowned and tipped my eyes away but not my head. He wouldn't let me. "What do you see?"

His thumb caressed my cheek, and he lowered his forehead to mine. The air between us mingled, as if he was buried inside me, and we were one body. "Nothing. No fire. No defiance. Only emptiness. And pain."

Surprised that he was so observant—the first man I'd

ever met who had a clue *and* paid attention—I closed my eyes to hide the stark grief his words cued in my body. I shuddered, icy cold dread making its way from the base of my spine to my lips. I licked them. "I'm worried about Ivy and Zenos."

It wasn't the truth, but it wasn't a lie either. I *was* worried for them, but it wasn't the top of my list.

Isaak wrapped me in his arms and pulled me even closer, used one hand to cradle my head to his chest. "Zenos is a Forsian hybrid, *gara*. Ivy looks human, but she has enough Hive tech in her body to make her nearly his equal in both speed and strength. Perhaps even more dangerous, but don't tell Zenos I said that. They are strong. I command you to cease your worrying."

At last, I smiled. "Command me to stop worrying? Pretty confident with those commands, aren't you? You should know a woman's heart does not work that way."

The comment made him freeze, his body becoming tense against mine. "And how does your heart work, *gara?*"

In his words, I heard something I'd never heard before... not from him. Vulnerability. Fear. I remained silent. I couldn't give him an answer when I didn't know myself. Didn't understand.

"I would know you," he said, his voice a husky whisper. No command, just honesty. "Know everything. Every hope and thought and dream. Every desire. Every need. I would know your heart, *gara*. If you would but allow it, I would make it mine."

I stopped breathing just for a moment. My mouth even fell open in surprise. "Isaak." I pushed at his chest, and he let me go. Stepping back, I looked up into his dark eyes and fought back the rising tide of hope that threatened to consume me. Hope, I had learned a long time ago, hurt more than almost any other emotion. Hope was a cruel bitch who never stayed. Like Isaak wouldn't once we were done with Bertok. He'd transport back to his spaceship to roam the galaxy. Damned rebel.

"I don't understand you," I said, looking out the window. "You want to go back to space, don't you? Back out there to hunt more Hive and sell more tech?"

"Yes. Of course," he said immediately. No hesitation or doubt. "I cannot stay here. My family—"

A loud ding interrupted us, and we turned to face the wall. Isaak hurried forward, pressing a panel. Part of the wall, of the stone itself, seemed to change before my eyes, turned into a flat screen. Ivy and Zenos appeared on the flat surface.

"Isaak of Trion. Please respond." Zenos's deep, rich tone would have been intimidating, but his voice was monotone. Completely under control.

"Damn it, Isaak. Answer the fucking phone." Ivy's irritated blast made me smile because I doubted Isaak knew what a phone was. That was more like it.

Isaak looked to me, as if asking permission, and I realized he was attempting to protect my modesty. I was clothed, but it did nothing to hide my body. But I'd watched some Trion broadcasts since our arrival. My gown was sheer, beautiful, and not unlike what every other woman on the planet wore. Oddly, I felt at home in the soft gown, despite how much desert air made its way up my skirts, so to speak. I simply nodded and moved to stand in front of the screen. Isaak touched the panel again and moved to stand beside me, his hand on the small of my back like I was his.

More torture, now that I realized how badly I wanted exactly that. Isaak. Mine. Forever. My master. My mate.

Yes. Hope. Still a heartless bitch.

"Zenos, Ivy, we are here."

"Thank God." Ivy leaned down as if she were speaking to a very small screen, her cute nose scrunched up as she squinted at us. "Nice dress, Zara. Trion looks good on you."

"Thank you." If I'd detected any sarcasm to her tone, I would have fired back. But she was sincere, the look in her eyes kind. "I really do like it here although I haven't seen much of the place."

"I bet Isaak's kept you occupied." I couldn't miss her sly grin. "I've heard Warden Egara really knows her stuff. I haven't met one unhappy Earth girl out here." Ivy blushed, and I wondered for a second why. Then she spoke. "Sorry. I shouldn't have said that. I forgot about your mate being murdered. You just look so perfect with Isaak that—"

"Female, enough drama and talk of mates. We have more important details to discuss." Zenos literally lifted her off her feet and pulled her backward and up into his arms, cradling her across his chest without the slightest sign of strain. And I'd met Ivy. She was six foot if she was an inch. But in her mate's arms she looked small.

Loved.

And happy. God, she gave in to his demands at once, settling her cheek against his shoulder and allowing him to hold her as he spoke of war and death and rage over the top of her golden head.

"It's been five weeks, Forsian. What took so long?" Isaak asked. The gentle tone he'd used with me was now gone.

Zenos' jaw clenched, and he glared at Isaak. "I can't just go to Cerberus legion and knock on the leader's door," he snapped. "We must listen, follow the movements of the legion's members. Have patience." He added the last intentionally.

Isaak didn't fall for it. "Well?"

"Astra gave us her assistance, and we tracked down the data source in that crystal," Isaak replied.

"And?" Isaak asked.

"We discovered plans for an attack on a city called Bakkarholt on Trion. As well as a date and time for the explosion."

Isaak stilled beside me. I couldn't even feel him breathing.

"Explosion?" It was my turn to freak out. "What kind of explosion?" Just my luck I'd find a place I loved, and some asshole alien would detonate a nuclear bomb or something on it. Hope really was a bitch, and she was cackling now.

"The attack is set to happen in four weeks. We had the computer calculate the time differential, and the attack on Bakkarholt will occur on Trion tomorrow afternoon, two hours past peak sun."

Ivy lifted her head. "That's Trion time, in case you were wondering. Not our time. Out here, it's almost a month away."

"*Fark*." Isaak paced the room now, and my back felt like ice without the heat of his touch.

I looked back to the screen. I didn't know where

Bakkarholt was, but it didn't matter.

"What about Bertok? I don't understand. Why would Cerberus blow up a city on Trion if they're working with Bertok?" Didn't make sense to me to blow up your own house or town.

Isaak answered instead of Zenos. "That city is not far from here. It's my father's territory. He and Bertok have never been friends. If Bertok can destroy Bakkarholt, he'll cripple my father's trade and take out the largest garrison of my father's fighters. The other Councilors would have no reason to suspect Bertok, and as the closest territory, he would be expected to assist us. Most likely to take over."

I snorted, I couldn't help it. "Assist you directly into the grave, right? So, he's doing a hostile takeover of your territory and using Cerberus to take the blame."

"Bertok will kill my father. Most likely force my mother to form an alliance once my father is dead."

"Bertok told me he's already got a mate," I said.

"Having several is allowed on Trion," Isaak replied absently.

I narrowed my gaze, wondered if he wanted multiple mates.

Perhaps he read my mind, for he said, "*Gara*, you are more than enough for me."

Ivy laughed. I whipped my head around and glared at her. I wasn't sure if I should be offended or pleased.

Isaak shook his head. "That scheming *fark*. He knows my father's position is weak."

"Why?" I looked around the room, the house that screamed money. Power.

Isaak was silent so long Zenos answered. "He has no

heir."

From what Isaak told me, his older brother had been heir, but he'd died. Isaak *was* the heir, but he'd been off-planet for years. He hadn't been here to step into his father's place if needed. From what he'd just said before the call about leaving Trion again, he never planned to. So, while there *was* an heir, there wasn't an heir who would take over. That was a lot of pressure on Isaak. What he wanted was different from what he might have to do if he wanted to save an entire fucking town.

Shit. I shifted my gaze from Isaak, who was running an agitated hand through his dark hair, to Zenos and Ivy.

"Can you send us the details of this plan?" I asked Zenos. "No one is going to believe a space pirate and an Earth girl who disappeared right after her new mate died. Knowing what I know about Bertok now, he probably found a way to frame me for Naron's murder. Why I left Trion so quickly after I arrived."

"Holy shit. I hadn't even thought about that." Ivy squirmed and Zenos gently settled her back on her feet, but she didn't break free. Instead, she leaned into him. His strength. His heat. She had her mate, her forever. I was standing here in Isaak's home, half naked and suddenly felt very alone.

"It's what I would have done." I crossed my arms over my chest and mentally kicked soft, pampered me to the curb. This wasn't my life. These weren't my clothes. You could take the girl away from the streets, but you couldn't take the streets out of the girl. Or something similar to that. "Destroy the city. Murder Isaak's father. Take out as many of his men as possible. He'll swoop in like a savior, make your mother trust him and take it all as his."

"We'll send you everything we have," Zenos said.

Isaak thanked them. "Tell Astra I owe her a favor."

Zenos laughed. "Don't think I will. She'd hold you to it, and that female never forgets anything. And her mate, Barek, is worse."

Another dinging noise sounded from the fancy screen, and Ivy looked at Isaak. "You get it?"

Isaak walked to the wall panel and pressed a few more buttons. "Yes. Thank you. I owe you both."

Ivy shook her head. "Take care of Zara. That's all. Earth girls stick together out here." Ivy glanced from Isaak to me. "If you need me, call me. We'll come. Got it?"

"Yes. Thanks." I meant that, with every cell in my body. They were helping us because they were friends. Because they were *good*. Because they cared not because they wanted something. They didn't have an ulterior motive.

With one last nod from both of them and a hard glare at Isaak from Zenos—which I didn't quite understand—they were gone.

"You need to call your father," I said.

"No, I don't." Isaak remained at the wall panel as data and maps began to appear and disappear on the large screen where Ivy and Zenos had been moments before.

"Look, I know you have some kind of family issue, but you have to call him. Or your mom. Somebody. We have to warn them."

He turned to look at me, the resignation in his gaze, the stiffness of his shoulders something I recognized well. He was bracing himself for pain.

"They're already here."

ara

MY BACK WENT RAMROD STRAIGHT, and I felt as if I were back on Earth and meeting a date's parents for the first time. Okay, that had never happened to me before, but I'd seen it in movies, and it was just as it had been depicted.

"They're here?" I couldn't miss the shrill tone of the question. I looked down at the sheer gown, the clearly visible nipple rings and chain, my bare feet. "Are you crazy? I can't meet your parents like this."

Isaak did something to make sure the screen was blank then turned and pulled me into his arms. It was supposed to be a reassuring gesture, I was sure, but it wasn't helping. "You look beautiful, *gara*. Perfect."

I blushed as much from his words as the heat in his eyes. "But—"

He put a finger over my lips. "No. You are perfect. They will not be allowed to believe otherwise."

I realized then that he hadn't seen his parents in years. Why was I panicking? There was a shit-ton of issues between them that I doubted I'd even register. How was he so calm?

A loud pounding sounded at the door before I could argue the obvious. He could not control his parents' thoughts—about him or me. And although I knew a bit about the rift that had driven Isaak from home, I knew from my own personal experience that family could be messy. He'd stayed away *four* years. That was messy.

And then there was the elephant in the room... Isaak was only on Trion to help me take care of Bertok. If he hadn't run into me, he'd never even have considered returning to his home planet. He wouldn't be facing his parents right now or ever. He was leaving again soon, going back out into space, for his ship and the freedom he seemed to need as much as he needed air.

He held me, and the pounding sounded at the door again.

"*Fark*, boy. Open the door before I have my guards blow it open." The voice was deep and commanding. Sounded like someone I knew all too well.

Isaak actually chuckled. "Patient, as always. Seems my father hasn't changed."

He released me and walked to the door, waved his hand over a panel and stood with his arms crossed over his chest as the door slid aside to reveal an older woman and a near exact copy of Isaak with a few more lines on his face.

Same stance. Same build. Same eyes.

Same scowl.

Isaak's skin had a richer tone than his father's, more like melted caramel, but the similarities between the two males startled me into a grin. Wow. Talk about strong genetics.

"Greetings, Father. Mother." Isaak inclined his head in a bit of a bow, and his mother rushed into his arms, an oomph escaping Isaak's chest from the impact.

"Isaak! I'm so glad you're home." He held her, a female just a bit taller than me, with dark brown curls and amber eyes. Her skin was darker than both her mate and son, as if she was from a different race or region of the planet. She had to be old enough to be Isaak's mother, but she didn't look a day over thirty. Not fair. But that wasn't what shocked me. No, what had me consciously closing my slack jaw was the see-through cream gown she wore. Even more revealing than mine, I could see everything, including the sparkling chains that ran between her breasts, the teardrop shaped diamonds —or something that looked just like diamonds— dangling about a half inch apart along the entire length. She wasn't supermodel thin, either. From what Isaak had said, she'd had given birth to at least one set of twins, and her body showed the signs. But she owned her body in a way I admired. She stood proudly, not an ounce of embarrassment or shame in her stance or her expression because she was scantily clad. No, she was covered completely but still exposed. Trion dress wasn't like skimpy, sexy lingerie. It was alluring yet modest. Carnal but protected.

Isaak had used the word adorned before. Well, she had that down. Besides the fancy chain, both of her arms were covered in gold and silver bangles so that every movement she made was accompanied by a faint tinkling sound like fairy bells. Her hair was pulled up into a loose style, and holding it in place was more bling, a circlet fit for any princess.

She looked like a fairy queen. Or a goddess... with her breasts showing.

"I did miss you, Mother." Isaak's tone was softer than I had ever heard before, and I was suddenly envious of this woman, of the love in Isaak's voice, of the way the guards and Isaak's father stood in a protective semi-circle around her, weapons out and at the ready to defend her. Then I realized they were all pointed at... me.

At last, she released her son and looked at him at arm's length. "You've been gone for over a month. And look at you! You're a man now. What have you been doing out there? Why didn't you come home sooner?"

A month?

Isaak told me he hadn't been home in *four years*. But then, Isaak and I had only been on Trion for just over a day and Ivy and Zenos said that out there, in space, it had been about 5 weeks. This Trion time difference thing was serious business. If it had only been a month, Isaak had been a man before he left. And now. Many adults didn't see their parents for a month or longer. Four years was a little extreme, but maybe it wasn't as bad as Isaak had made it out to be.

Isaak's father had his arms crossed again. "Captain Erick, take the female into custody. Then we will deal with my rebellious son."

Or maybe it was just as bad. Or worse.

"Yes, Councilor Henrick." One of the biggest, sexiest

aliens I had ever seen stepped forward, around Isaak and his mother, and approached me.

"What?" I set a hand on my chest. "Me? Is this supposed to be a joke? Because it's not funny." Holy fucking shit. Seriously? I left Earth to get away from gangs and crime and a bullshit existence, and the first time I set foot on Trion, my mate was murdered in front of me. And the second time they wanted to arrest me? If it had been a month since Isaak had been gone, then it had been maybe a day on Trion since I'd transported from Earth?

"What are you talking about, Father?" Isaak stepped back from his mother as Captain Erick and two additional guards moved around him and toward me.

It was Isaak's mother who answered. "She's dangerous, son. Killed her mate, Naron. Both his brother and Councilor Bertok are demanding justice."

Bertok? Did she just say Bertok? I took a step back and sputtered. "No. This is a huge mistake."

Captain Erick stepped closer and despite the fact that I was trying to be strong, I looked to Isaak for help. Was he going to stick his neck out to help me? Sure, he'd brought me here, but family was family, and I wasn't that. He wouldn't defy his father, the Councilor. I remembered that term because Bertok was one as well. Clearly Isaak's dad was just as important as Bertok. Most likely Councilors stuck together. No one had ever tried to protect me. Not in my whole life. Not my deadbeat father who disappeared when I was a kid and not my mother who'd always been more interested in her latest boyfriend to waste energy worrying about me. Or protecting me. Or standing up for me.

Earth. Trion. It was all the same.

"I need you to come with me, Zara Novak of Earth." Captain Erick stood before me now, blocking my view of Isaak, his father and his mother. Which was just as well. I wasn't going to run down the street half naked, with bare feet on a planet I knew nothing about. I had nowhere to go. I could get my one phone call and try to get in touch with Zenos and Ivy, but I doubted they'd be up for breaking me out of Trion jail. And were they my friends or Isaak's?

I was too tired and heartbroken at the moment to keep fighting.

I'd been alone on Earth. I was alone in space. I would always be alone. Shit happened. I should use the S-Gen machine and put it on a t-shirt.

"I didn't kill him." I held out my hands, wrists up and waited for whatever the Trion version of handcuffs was to close around my flesh. "Don't you people have video cameras or something? It happened at a transport center. I'd only just arrived from Earth. Naked. It wasn't like I brought something with me from Earth. You don't have any security footage to check?"

Captain Erick shook his head. "The comm system was disabled the day of your arrival."

"That's convenient." It was my word against Bertok's.

"Apologies, my lady." The captain reached for my wrists, and I blinked back tears. This sucked. But had I really expected anything different? I was not the fairy-tale, happy ending kind of girl.

The first touch of the dark gray restraint was cold against my skin, and I blew out a breath. Closed my eyes, but a growl and a funny *eep* sound had them popping open.

Captain Erick went flying, as in across the room, three feet off the ground, flying. Before me stood Isaak. He lifted a hand to my cheek. "Are you all right, *gara?*"

I couldn't answer. I was paralyzed. Shock? Rage? Fear? Relief? I had no idea how to feel. "What are you doing? Why did you do that? Now you're in trouble."

"My parents are used to me being defiant. It is not new. No one is taking you anywhere." He pulled me into his arms, and I went willingly, shocked that he had defended me, was protecting me against his own family. He turned his head, looked at his father. "She is innocent. You will not touch her."

"Son, be reasonable for once in your life." Isaak's father didn't raise his voice, which somehow made his chastisement worse. In my arms, Isaak stiffened. Captain Erick was back on his feet, space gun drawn and pointed at Isaak.

"*Fark* reasonable," Isaak countered. "Councilor Bertok murdered Naron, sold Zara to Cerberus and, even now, plots to destroy Bakkarholt." Isaak moved us both, placing me behind him when Captain Erick took a step forward. "Don't do it, Erick. We grew up together. You were like a brother to me. But if you touch her again, I'll kill you."

"Isaak!" His mother's voice was full of shock.

"I mean it, Mother. Zara is innocent, and she has suffered enough."

"She has not been claimed, son. She has not been adorned."

Yeah, that had been obvious when my own nipples

had been on full display. I'd *told* Isaak I couldn't let his parents see me this way. But noooo.

"You have no right to place her under your protection." His father's deep voice still had not changed. Condescending, that's what I would call it. Like he was explaining things to a child, as if he was used to doing this with Isaak.

"Think about what Bertok is spreading about her. She transported from Earth, and Naron was dead within minutes."

Isaak looked to me for confirmation. I nodded.

"How would she get to The Dome? Why would she even go there? She was a processed bride not a Coalition volunteer. She was matched to Naron through the testing. She had no idea she would even be matched to Trion."

I'd first thought there'd been a mistake being matched to this planet. Now I needed to send the warden a thank you note. Although my troubles weren't behind me yet.

"If what you say is true, Naron's brother would be her protector now," Isaak's father said.

Naron had a brother? And by Trion law I would belong to him? Or if not belong to as his mate but be under his family's control? They called it protection, but I knew the truth. Isaak stood fully clothed, as did his father. His mother and I? Half naked. Dressed like this, we wouldn't be able to fight our way out of a paper bag. My fingers itched for my titan stick. *That* would get the guys to see me differently.

For the space of a few seconds, I thought this would be the moment Isaak claimed me as his mate. This would be when he confessed that he had feelings for me, that what was between us was more than just sex. That he'd come back to Trion for more than just being a rebel.

"I gave her my word that I would keep her safe and help her bring justice to Bertok," he told them.

That was not romantic. Not at all. And now I was blinking back tears for an all new and more painful reason. A reason I shouldn't be considering.

Isaak didn't want a future with me. He wanted to get this thing with Bertok done and go back out into space to hunt his robot parts and live on that tiny little spaceship.

I didn't want that. I wanted a home. A family. I wanted to take walks with my kids and look for butterflies—assuming they had something like that on Trion. I wanted a new life. Something completely different than the shitshow I'd struggled through on Earth.

I wanted Isaak, but what was that stupid saying? *Want in one hand, shit in the other.*

At least I wasn't going to be hauled off to jail. Yet.

That would have to do for now.

I'd make sure Bertok was punished for Naron's death, say good-bye to Isaak, and worry about the rest later. I would survive. That was what I knew. That was the one thing I was good at. I'd survive. I always did.

saak

BEHIND ME, Zara shook. I had seen the sheen of tears in her eyes, watched her shoulders droop as my father's captain of the guard, my boyhood friend, Erick, had moved toward her. In the moment her gaze lifted to mine, I'd seen something I never wanted to see in her beautiful eyes again when she looked at me. Disappointment. Pain. Resignation.

Even when she'd stood beside Jirghogis, she'd looked fierce and determined.

Here, now, she had believed I was going to allow her to be taken. I had hesitated for a split second, but that had been enough to betray her trust. *Fark*!

My father's scowl deepened, but he wisely waved Erick away from me when the brute would have come at me again. "You are making very serious accusations against an extremely powerful Councilor, Isaak. A Councilor who also happens to be one of my strongest allies." There it was—the censure. The judgment. The disbelief. His trust in this was in Bertok not me. His son. He believed the lies a politically grasping Councilor said over his own blood.

As usual, my mother remained silent. In private, she would scream and rant when the mood took her. But in public, before our people or our guards, she was always the dutiful and submissive female. The perfect Trion mate.

"What he says is true. You don't have to believe me, but Isaak's your son," Zara said. "You shouldn't need proof in order to believe him."

Zara moved to stand beside me, and her words fell into a deafening and shocked silence. They might have echoed my thoughts, but I doubted my father had ever been spoken to in such a manner, in public, and by an unclaimed female. But gods, I was glad to see her fire back. She didn't have much hope for herself, but when it came to standing up for me...*fark*. What a fierce and stunning female she was.

"Zara." I warned her with my tone not because I didn't admire her spirit but because I did not want my father to direct his wrath at her. He could speak to me in any manner he chose. I'd walked away from it once, and I planned to do so again. I was very practiced at ignoring him. But I would not have him threatening Zara.

"No, Isaak." Zara stepped forward to stand even closer to my parents. "Your son is honorable and brave. He has saved my life more than once and sacrificed a lot to do so. You will not be mean to him in front of me."

Be mean to me?

My mother closed the distance until the two females stood facing one another, toes nearly touching. I glanced at my father, uncertain how to proceed. I would never dare lay a hand on my mother, not even to gently pull her away from Zara. And Zara? If I interfered now, she'd probably want to jab me with her titan stick.

"Zara, I am Eela. It is an honor to meet you. Captain, take the restraints from her." Erick took a step their way but paused. He answered to my father. "Now," she added. The words held no command, but Erick did her bidding, removing the cuffs from Zara's wrists before stepping back.

"The honor is mine." Zara held out her hand in what I assumed was some kind of human custom. My mother looked confused then reached out with both of her hands to take hold of Zara's.

Both ladies smiled until Zara spoke again. "Ma'am, I'm serious. Do not disrespect your son in front of me." She looked up to glare at my father. "Either of you. It's not his fault Malik died. I'm so sorry for your loss, but he lost someone too. His twin. He might not be the kind to sit behind a desk and talk politics, but if he hadn't been out there, in space, I'd be with Cerberus right now and your precious city wouldn't' stand a chance. You should be on your knees thanking him for being rebellious. Bertok's one scary old guy and isn't what you think. Isaak's rebel ass is about to save a lot of lives."

My father stared at Zara like she had three heads. My mother's eyes widened, clearly stunned by her earthly manners. Laughter flowed into the silence like magic.

"Oh, Isaak. I like this one. I approve of your choice in mate."

"Oh, I'm not—I mean, Isaak is going to go back to space as soon as this Bertok thing is over." Zara's halting words reminded me that she was not mine. She had refused to call me master. Even now, she did not allow me to care for her, instead speaking out against my father directly. It was obvious she still did not trust me, had not given herself into my care, and there was nothing I could do to force her to accept me. She was not wrong. I had no intention of staying on Trion. My father's stern frown solidified that truth. I was not wanted here. Not really.

I was the wrong son.

If Malik had come to father with Bertok's scheme, he would have been believed instantly, without question.

"If you have proof, Son, present it now. I have a Councilor's meeting to attend, and Bertok will be there."

"No," I commanded. "You can't go."

"Give me a reason not to," my father insisted.

Fark.

My comm rang once more, and I turned from the drama in my living area to the screen on the wall. With a wave of my hand, Zenos and Ivy appeared.

Zenos took in everyone around me within two seconds then looked to me. "Isaak, Cerberus is on the move. I'm tracking the attack ship. It will be within range of Trion within the hour. That's your time, by the way. We had the computer figure out the difference."

My father moved closer to the screen and inspected Zenos and Ivy. "Who are you? I see the mark of Astra legion on your arm. Why are you communicating with my son?"

My father knew of the Rogue 5 legions?

Zenos ignored him as Ivy leaned around to look for Zara. As if she were in the room with us and trying to get my father out of the way. "Hey Zara, you good? We can be there in a few days, which is like ten hours for you. Get you off that rock if they aren't treating you right."

A sharp protest was on my lips, but my father beat me to it. "Trion males worship their mates, female. Do not insult my son again."

If he expected Ivy—from Earth—to back down, he was about to be disappointed.

"Zara is my friend," she countered. "No offense, but I don't know you. So, if you would kindly move out of my way, I'd like to hear from Zara directly. Otherwise, Zenos and I will come down there and cause problems you don't want."

Behind me, Zara chuckled. My mother gasped. I had no idea what my father's reaction would be, but he looked at Zenos and Ivy on the screen. "I assume, female, that you and Zara Novak are from the same planet?"

Ivy's grin was pure mischief. "You know it. Earth girls don't put up with bullshit, so please let me talk to Zara."

Zara moved forward. "I'm fine, Ivy. I promise. Thank you for wanting to come to my rescue. It means more than you'll ever know."

Ivy whistled. "Whoa, woman. You've gone full native with that outfit."

Zara smiled, but it didn't reach her eyes. "It's temporary. Once Bertok is taken care of, Isaak is heading your way. He's got more tech to hunt."

She frowned. "What?"

"He's going back to being a space pirate, and I'll be going home."

It was Zenos' turn to frown. "To Earth?"

I looked away from the screen and to watch Zara. She nodded. "Yes. I can't stay here."

She was stating the impossible. No female from the Bride Program could return to her home planet. My father was correct. She was under Naron's brother's protection. She would go to live with them.

The urge to reach for her and pull her into my arms was strong, but there wasn't time. I would deal with the attack on Bakkarholt, take care of Bertok, and once Zara and my father's people were safe, I would speak with the stubborn female. She belonged on Trion. Her response to me was proof of that. The way she reveled in the Trion culture was something she needed, something the testing pulled from her and showed her. Even if she wasn't with me.

Zenos's deep, no-nonsense voice penetrated the fog in my mind. "Forty-nine minutes, Isaak."

"What is going on?"

I spun on my heel and faced my father. "Bertok killed Zara's mate and traded her to Cerberus. In exchange, Cerberus legion is on their way here to blow up the entire city of Bakkarholt."

Mother gasped, and Father's jaw clenched at the words.

"Cerberus doesn't care if the blame falls on him. He's known for worse crimes. Cerberus wants an Earth female. Bertok wants control of another region. Bertok heard of Naron's match and found exactly what Cerberus wanted, took her. Sold her. Cerberus staging the attack will only make him more ruthless and infamous across the galaxy."

Father blinked, processed my words. Realized the implications. With Trion being so remote, the planet didn't have much interaction with others. The fact that Cerberus from distant Rogue 5 wanted to destroy an entire city was difficult to comprehend. It was solely because of Zara, really. If she'd been matched to a different planet, perhaps Viken, then it was possible she'd have been sold to Cerberus just the same, but there would have been no bargain to wreak devastation on Trion. Even so, she was innocent. Father had to see that it was Bertok who was the true villain in this.

"Do you have a stealth ship I can borrow?" I asked. "I can't keep trying to get you to believe me. I don't even care if you don't. I'm not going to let Bakkarholt be destroyed and tens of thousands of Trion people die."

He shook his head. "No. Your ship is where you left it, as is your brother's. Captain Erick?"

"Yes, sir?"

"Get your men on Malik's ship," Father ordered. "Isaak and I will take the other fighter. We will send you coordinates as soon as we are on board."

My mother placed her hand on Father's shoulder. "I will take the remaining guards and go to Outpost None. I will hold your seat at the council meeting until you arrive. Hopefully, you will return with the proof we need to prosecute Bertok and eliminate the threat to our people."

My mother believed me. *Fark.*

I turned to Zara. "You will go with my mother, Zara. Remain out of sight, *gara,* and stay with the guards until I arrive." It was a command, nothing less. I knew what she was capable of. The Omega Dome was one thing, but Trion another entirely. Women were revered and cherished, but they also didn't behave as Zara would in a dangerous situation. But at least Outpost Nine should be safe. The tent city moved around the planet to host meetings among the High Councilors of the various Trion regions. The Outpost was always heavily guarded and rarely in the same place twice.

Zara tilted her head, and I had no idea if she would obey me or not. I was not her master. She had made that very clear. "Fine. But I'm keeping the cattle prod."

I nodded. It was a wise idea. She was skilled with the titan stick, and I would feel better knowing she was armed.

"Good luck, friends," Zenos said from the screen. "I look forward to seeing Cerberus' plans defeated and a traitor on your planet brought to justice."

"Tell Astra I'm taking down this Cerberus ship for her. Tell her she owes me one."

Zenos chuckled, the deep rumble easing a mood that had begun to feel suffocating. "I like the way you bargain, pirate. Consider it done."

A few quick commands on the comm system, and I transferred the data Zenos and Ivy had sent me to my old ship, relieved to discover that my father had told the truth. My ship and its command codes were intact, exactly as I had left it. We just had to go to the landing bay to climb aboard.

"Let's go, Father."

"You have allies on Rogue 5?"

"Yes." I was already moving, grabbing gear.

"What else have you been doing out there?" My father's tone made me pause, as I heard a bit of mirth behind the question. And perhaps...approval?

No. Now was not the time to indulge in wishful thinking. "Priorities, father. Bakkarholt. Bertok." I glanced at Zara, who stood stoically, waiting to leave with my mother. "Then we'll talk about the rest."

"Agreed." My father waved Erick ahead. "Go, Captain. Now. We're right behind you." While he knew how to fly a craft, I'd rarely known him to do it. He fought battles diplomatically not in space with weapons. We had to intercept Cerberus' ship, had to keep him from destroying Bakkarholt. We couldn't do it from the ground. He was a wise man and knew what needed to be done. He just had to believe it was actually happening.

Father and Mother embraced briefly, and I touched Zara on the cheek. "Behave, *gara*. Do not place yourself in danger. I will return."

The guards left with Erick until it was just the four of us, my parents, Zara and me. "I will not leave Zara unprotected like this father."

"Don't worry, Isaak. You should know your father better than that." My mother was smiling as she moved to the door. Opened it.

Half a dozen guards stood outside. My mother's personal guards. They fought for the right to protect her every year in a tournament. It was the most exalted position in my father's army, and he paid them very, very well.

I traced the line of Zara's cheek and pretended her smile was real. She would be safe.

It wasn't much, but it was all I could give her.

14

SITTING in the pilot's seat of my favorite fighter, Malik's identical ship visible on my flight screen, I finally felt like I had come home.

My father's silence from the seat next to me was all too familiar as well, so I chose to ignore it and addressed Erick through the comms rather than fumble my way through awkward conversation with a male who clearly did not wish to speak to me. I'd never once flown with him, learning from instructors or by pure seat-of-the-pants instinct.

"Coordinates transmitted, Erick. Verify," I said.

"Verified. What's the plan, Isaak?" There he was, my old friend. If he touched Zara again, I'd have to rethink his role. Out here, flying, I was in command, but we were more than soldiers to one another. We had always been close, me, Malik, and Erick. Brothers of a sort. The familiar tenor of his voice made me realize there were things on Trion I had missed. I'd walked away from more than my parents.

"Destroy them," I told him, steering us around the nearest asteroid belt to where the Cerberus ship was. "No prisoners. No mercy. They are here to kill our people. We take them out by whatever means necessary."

I'd fought the Hive before. Not as a fighter but as a rebel. I'd never once considered the Cerberus legion to be an enemy. Most steered clear while I was aiming my ship right for them.

My father made a noise that sounded like a groan, but this was not up for debate. Cerberus wanted Zara for himself. No *farking* way that was happening. He was going to destroy a city on Trion. No *farking* way that was happening either. If I didn't stop him, no one would. It would be too late for any Trion military to put up defenses.

I needed the leader of one of the most notorious Rogue 5 legions to hear me loud and clear. Go after Zara, you die.

Go after my people, you die.

In this, Zara was correct. I was not my brother. I would not negotiate. *Fark* that, I wouldn't even listen to people from such a vile criminal organization. I was not a diplomat or a politician, I was a hunter, a killer, a warrior without mercy if someone threatened what was mine.

But then, Zara wasn't truly mine. Neither was Trion... not anymore. But I buried those thoughts. They were not for now. Later, I would deal with the fallout of this fight. Later, I would deal with my father's disapproval and my mother's sorrow because this time. I would leave, and they would know the true reason. While we all mourned Malik still, the truth couldn't hide behind his loss. Right now, I had to protect them all.

"I have nothing on my scanners. Are you sure this is the right place?" Erick asked.

"Yes. Trust me. They're here." I reached forward and adjusted my ship's scanners to a frequency that would detect the stealth technology I was sure the Cerberus ship was using. Zenos had it, could see them. He was used to the Hive tech. I knew because I'd sold it to them. "Adjust your scanners to match mine. You won't see the ship, more like a shadow."

"*Fark.* I see it." Erick sounded shocked. My father leaned forward in the co-pilot's seat and reached for the controls.

"Targeting their ship's engines." My father's nimble fingers moved over the controls with a practiced ease that reminded me he'd once served in the Coalition Fleet, that he'd been a fighter before becoming a diplomat. That my mother, like Zara, was an Interstellar Bride.

"Don't activate the ion cannon yet," I told him. "As soon as you lock on target, they'll know we can see them, and they'll attack."

"They could fire on Bakkarholt at any moment." There was no censure in my father's voice, mere statement of fact.

He was right, but we could not destroy their ship, not yet. "We need them to set their target before we take them out. We need proof to take down Bertok. He's too powerful and has too many friends on Trion. Just being here isn't enough."

"It's a risk."

"A necessary risk, Father. Trust me, Bertok is too dangerous. We have to finish this."

Patient as a spider, my father sat with his hands hovering over the controls. "Agreed."

"Intercept in two minutes. Target acquired but not locked," Erick reported.

"Perfect. They won't lock on to Bakkarholt until we fly past their ship. They think we can't see them. Be ready to reverse course and fire immediately from the rear. If we're fast enough, we'll catch them with their shielding down."

Erick mumbled through the comms, just as eager as I to end the enemy. "Trust me, we're ready."

The longest two minutes of my life ensued as I watched the Cerberus ship grow closer and closer. But they were smart. Sneaky. They did not activate their ion cannon. They did not activate their targeting systems. They flew like a ghost ship. Had Zenos and Ivy not warned us, there would have been no way to stop them. None.

We flew past them as if out for a practice run. No hurry. No shielding. No weapons. Two ships flying a routine patrol.

"Get ready." I inspected the Cerberus ship as we flew by. It was twice the size of the ship I flew and loaded with three times the weapons. "Don't miss, Erick. They've got enough firepower to take out a small fleet."

"Holy gods, what the *fark* is that?" Erick's shock had my father leaning forward.

"Drift up, son. Get a closer look."

I followed Father's words, so I could get a good look at the top of the Cerberus ship.

"That *farking* Xeriman. She bought my Spectra IV." The irony was not lost on me. There, mounted atop the Cerberus ship was the Spectra IV ion cannon I had ordered from the Silver Scions. I knew it was mine because I had requested a special insignia be embossed on the side of the cannon. My family crest.

"Is that... is that our crest?" Father asked, wide eyed.

"That was to be mine."

"You negotiated with the enemy?"

I looked to him, his gaze serious and dark.

"You negotiate with the enemy, Father. What I've done is diplomacy. Watched. Listened. *Fark,* if I hadn't been selling to them, we wouldn't be here right now saving the planet.

Father listened, studied me, then nodded.

I didn't know what it meant, but it wasn't hurtful words.

"She probably used my money to buy it."

Now Ulza, or one of her sons, was probably on that ship. And they intended to use *my* Spectra IV to kill an entire city full of people.

"What is a Spectra IV?" Erick asked through the head set.

"It's a specialty cannon built with Hive tech. They could take out a city five times the size of Bakkarholt with that cannon."

"And what were you going to do with an ion cannon with our family crest emblazoned on the side?" My father's voice was deadly quiet, and I knew the sight had angered him as nothing else might have.

"Because it's mine. I ordered that cannon to help me

hunt and kill Hive. I didn't have a weapon big enough to take down their Integration ships."

"By the gods, son. You've spent the last four years hunting Hive? On your own?"

There it was, the criticism. The disbelief. The blatant *disapproval.*

The Cerberus ship saved me from the need to respond. "They're locking on target."

"I see it." Now that their weapons were activated, our ships could detect the signals. I frowned. "Something's not right. They're going the wrong..."

"*Fark.* They've locked onto Outpost Nine." My father's skin paled. "Eela."

"What?" Shocked, I double checked my father's data. "*Fark.* Zara."

"Why would they--?" Erick made a choking sound as he answered his own question. "The High Councilors' meeting."

"They're taking out Bertok. He didn't hold up his end of their bargain. Fire, Erick! Do it now. Take them out!" I shoved my father's shocked hand out of the way and fired everything I had at the Cerberus ship's engines from the back, their flank.

Confident Erick would keep up the tirade, I shifted my target to the glowing Spectra IV ion cannon on top of the Cerberus ship. "*Fark* you, Ulza. That cannon has to be mounted internally." I knew because I had helped the engineer working with the Silver Scions to design it. The cannon was insanely powerful but had one major weakness near the center top panel. The cannon couldn't withstand a direct shot, which was why I had redesigned my ship to create a housing for it that would protect the body of the cannon from Hive attack.

I had no problem with Cerberus finishing Bertok. There was a decent line of people waiting for a turn. But my mate was at the meeting. My mother. Use my *farking* cannon to kill *my mate!*

Everything around me faded to blank space. Nothing existed but the Cerberus ship and that cannon.

I fired my weapons, adjusted, fired again.

"Direct hit!" Erick yelled the news, but I already knew. I'd known from the moment I fired the shot and waited, watched it explode into the ion cannon as if my entire existence was happening in ultra-slow motion. Zara was down there. If I missed the shot, Zara would die.

You can't outrun pain...

Her truth hit me hard, like a punch to my gut. I couldn't breathe. If I lost her, there would be nowhere to run. Nowhere to hide. There weren't enough Hive in the universe to erase the agony losing her would be. I could travel the galaxy like I had been the past four years, but I'd never find what made me happy.

I'd rather be dead.

The Cerberus ship exploded into tiny pieces, and I watched with satisfaction as they fell toward Trion, burning up in the planet's atmosphere like a meteor storm.

I was an idiot.

"Outpost Nine, Erick. Now."

"Right behind you."

I didn't look at my father, but I could feel his assessment, his eyes burning into me in the way only a stern parent's could.

I no longer cared. Zara. I had to get to Zara.

The ion cannon was gone, but Bertok? That asshole was down there, on the surface, with my mate.

My father leaned forward to activate the comms.

"What are you doing?"

He grinned, the happy look in his eyes one I hadn't seen in years. "I am notifying the council that there is a traitor in their midst, and that my brilliant, fearless son just saved them all."

Brilliant? Fearless?

"Your female was right, Isaak. The years away have made you smarter. Stronger. Your brother was kind and funny, but he was soft. Weak. I loved him, but our people will fare very well under your protection."

Once, I would have sold my soul to hear such praise from my father's lips. Now? I needed to reach Zara. I cared about nothing else.

"Thank you, father." Simple words, but I had nothing else to say.

ara

"THEY WILL NOT LET US WITHIN," Eela said.

We walked down a grand hallway in some fancy building. Just outside were a group of tents, and outside those tents stood dozens of armed guards.

Inside the building, which would put any stone castle on Earth to shame, there wasn't anyone around, and I had to assume everyone was in the meeting. I didn't know where we were because I'd only been in the transport station and then in Isaak's house for the duration of my time on Trion. We were obviously in a town, a desert town where Isaak's dad was the head guy. They called them Councilors. Bertok was one for his area. Perhaps like governors or presidents of different parts of the planet.

Now wasn't time to have a civics lesson about the place, but I didn't understand Eela's statement.

"Why not?"

We had three guards with us. They loomed and looked somewhat frightening, but she didn't pay them any attention. As for me, I wasn't used to protection. To being supervised. I wasn't used to wearing a see-through dress either. I'd changed a lot.

One thing that hadn't changed was that I wasn't going to listen to what Isaak or anyone else said. I wasn't being defiant, I was doing what I needed to do. Staying out of sight and trying to be safe was a good idea, but it wasn't going to get the job done. And that job was to see Bertok taken down.

I wasn't going to do that from Isaak's posh mansion.

Thankfully, Eela knew that too.

That was why we were here. Wherever that was. All I knew was there was a Councilor meeting, and Isaak's dad was supposed to be a part of it. Same went for Bertok.

"Why not?" I asked. We had three big goons, and I had my titan stick.

"Females are not allowed in these meetings alone. Not that I wish to attend. I sat through several meetings after I took Henrick as my mate. The pillow was comfortable, but the conversation was very boring."

I turned to face her, the closed door behind me. "Okay, we've got to work on this females-not-allowed thing. There aren't any female Councilors?"

She shook her head.

"Don't you want to have representation?"

She gave me a smile. A sly one. "I do have representation. My mate sits up on the council."

"Yeah, but *you* could sit there yourself."

She gave a slight shrug of her dark shoulders. Her skin practically glowed. At a later date, I'd have to ask her about her lotion.

"Males give their ear to their mates. And their voice."

I stared at her, tried to figure out what she meant. "You mean... pillow talk?"

She quirked her lips. "Males like to *think* they are in charge, but it is the females who truly run this planet."

"But Bertok is planning on blowing up a huge city. Are you saying his wife gave him a hummer and told him to do it?"

Her eyes widened. "I have not heard the term hummer before, but I can imagine. It is possible, but I know his mate. She would not be so cruel or cunning. I would assume there is evil on Earth as well."

I nodded. "It is why I volunteered."

She laughed then covered her mouth with her fingers. "I'm sorry. It isn't funny. You've been through much. Isaak, I assume, was not keen to return to Trion. He and his father have always clashed. But here he is. Because of you. And perhaps... a hummer?"

I didn't convince Isaak to return to Trion because of a blowjob, but I wasn't going to mention that in any way to Isaak's mom. Not a chance. She might be able to see my nipples, but I wasn't telling her about my sex life with her son.

"If we can't get in, then why did you say you would hold the council off until your mate could return? Wouldn't it have been better to get on that ship with Isaak and have Isaak's father sit in on the meeting?"

"I do not care for space travel. I become unwell. I am needed here."

"Then how do we get in?" I wondered.

"We open the door."

She went over to the closed door and opened it, walked inside, two of the three guards following her. The third remained with me. I glanced up at him, but his expression was neutral.

I wasn't sure if Eela was ballsy or what. It was time to find out.

I followed her in to find a bunch of guys in white robes like weird sheiks standing about squawking like pigeons, offended that Eela was there. The room was arranged in a U shape, with three tiers of chairs that all faced the door. It was as if we'd walked into the men's locker room by mistake and caught them all with their pants down.

Eela stood poised and calm. Well, I assumed she did, since I couldn't see her around the guards. But she remained quiet and let the roomful of guys make their noise. She must have raised her hand or flashed a boob or something because they all fell silent.

"Right now, Cerberus from Rogue 5 is within striking distance of Trion with the intention of destroying Bakkarholt."

Pandemonium broke out.

Again, Eela waited. The males in the room were a variety of ages, but they leaned toward the gray-haired crowd. I took them all in, calmly inspecting faces until I saw Bertok. I froze. He was two rows up and directly at the back of the room. He looked exactly as I remembered, wearing the same outfit. His gaze was direct and dark. I recognized the glare well as he'd pierced me with it before. He wasn't pleased with Eela or her announcement but remained silent.

"Where is this information coming from?" A Councilor asked from our right.

"It matters not, and you will not believe me. You wish for proof. Comm the central command and have them ping the space defense patrols."

The guy looked like he had indigestion at the idea of taking orders from a female. The guy nodded to someone beside him, and the second male started speaking into a wristwatch or what looked like one.

"Where is your mate, my lady?" another guy asked. "High Councilor Henrick should be here to share this revelation himself."

"It matters not whether the news is from a male's or female's lips. The truth is the same. Bakkarholt will be destroyed within the hour. As for where my mate is, he is with our son, fighting the Cerberus craft in space."

Shouting began again. I watched Bertok. He didn't say a word.

This wasn't getting anywhere fast. Perhaps that was Eela's plan. Stall and stall some more.

Eela might be here to delay the meeting.

I was here to take down Bertok.

I stepped around the guards and moved to stand beside Eela. The room grew quiet again. I, too, waited, but for something different. I waited for Bertok to speak. I knew he would. He had to.

"Arrest her! She is the fugitive bride who murdered her matched mate. She killed Naron, one of my guards."

The protection behind us didn't stir, our guards impervious to Bertok's lies.

"How did I kill him, Bertok?" I shouted, speaking over the din of voices. They silenced instantly.

"You sliced his throat." He stepped down from his tier of seats and made his way to the main floor where Eela and I stood. He slowly walked in our direction.

"With what? Interstellar Brides arrive on Trion bare, without clothing or weapons. Surely you are not so ignorant that you are not aware of this custom?" I took my time, my gaze clashing with every male within view before I continued. "Surely, males of such high regard are not *all so* ignorant of their planet's customs."

I heard a funny sound from Eela, but she remained quiet. If females could guide their mates by pillow talk, I could get what I wanted by pricking their vanity or male pride. These were all leaders of the planet.

They all took offense by my statement.

"Naron's death was recorded at four minutes after transport of his mate," someone from our left called out.

"She could have found a knife in that time."

"Even if I did kill him, I couldn't return to Earth. I'm now under the protection of Naron's family. I believe his brother is the male head. Why would I kill my mate, my matched mate, knowing I would be forced to go live with his family?"

"You fled immediately. Trion intelligence reported your presence at Omega Dome, in Sector Zero. If we are about to be attacked by Cerberus, as you claim, it is most likely at your bidding, treacherous female."

"Earth is a new member of the Coalition. No one

from Earth even knows of the Omega Dome's existence. No one."

Bertok stopped about fifteen feet in front of me, hands folded in front of him like a creepy, old priest.

"Leave her be, Bertok. She is small. A female." One of the other Councilors stepped forward. "I met Naron. This female is incapable of defeating him."

The conversation seemed to be turning in my favor, so I resisted the urge to argue. I knew how to fight dirty. I *could* murder a man Naron's size, if I had the element of surprise and got lucky. But that didn't mean I had.

"It is a Councilor's duty to protect the planet from danger, including those of the lying, female variety."

I cocked my head to the side. "If I was so dangerous, why did you sell me to Cerberus? Why did you trade me, a human female, for his assistance in destroying an opposing region's city?"

Murmurs swirled around us.

"What city?" someone asked.

"Bakkarholt." Eela spoke up from behind me and shouts erupted at her response.

"Two Trion fighters have engaged a Cerberus attack ship in Trion air space." The announcement came from the guy who'd spoken into his wrist watch.

The silence was deafening as everyone absorbed the news. I didn't wait to press my advantage. "Cerberus is here because Bertok arranged it. He used me to deliver the coordinates of Bakkarholt through a necklace. I'm not up on my Trion politics, but what would happen if that city was destroyed?"

All eyes turned to Bertok as the other Councilors considered the answer.

"And what would happen to Cerberus if he was blamed for the attack?"

"Nothing," Eela said, her voice loud and clear. "Everyone knows his evil legion can't be stopped. Only the Coalition Fleet would have the firepower to destroy them, and they are too busy fighting a war."

"This female speaks nonsense. She murdered her mate and fled to Omega Dome."

"Careful with your lies, Bertok. Are you sure Cerberus will really fire upon Bakkarholt? I mean, you messed up. You promised Cerberus a bride from Earth. But I'm here and not on Rogue 5. You didn't uphold your end of the bargain. What happens when you break your word with Cerberus legion? Maybe he sent a ship here for retribution. What we call *payback* on Earth. Maybe they're here to kill you."

It was a bluff. I had no idea what Cerberus was going to do. But if Bertok freaked out and tried to save his own ass, then everyone in the room would know the truth. As no one moved to stop me or interrupt, I assumed they were waiting for Bertok's reaction as well.

"Cerberus is here for you, Bertok. You. They don't care about Bakkarholt," I repeated. "What's the biggest city in your region? Maybe they'll be satisfied with blowing up your house? Maybe they'll track you through your comm system and send assassins? But they're here. You should probably say goodbye to your family and friends."

His eyes widened, and he turned his back to me. Speaking into his own wrist device as he spun on his heel, he started walking toward a door at the back of the chamber. "Sound the alarms in the Wildlands. Danger level five. Threat imminent."

"Guards, seize Councilor Bertok!" one of the men shouted.

The guards nearest Bertok were the protection trio who'd come in with us. They started to move, but I was closer to Bertok. I wasn't going to miss the opportunity to take him down.

I ran for him, spun my titan stick around in an arc and lunged, zapping the guy in the ass.

He startled, stiffened and let out a high-pitched yelp. Turning, he glared at me. "You! You ruined it all!"

There was the asshole I remembered. Now I'd let every other Councilor see the man behind the curtain.

"Yeah, I'm not all that meek, am I? I'm just what Cerberus wants, except your plan didn't work."

The guards flanked me but wisely exercised caution about approaching Bertok with me waving my titan stick around.

"The only place you're going to be ruling over is prison."

His face turned dark red and veins popped out at his temple. He was one pissed off old asshole.

"Outpost Nine, this is High Councilor Henrick." A deep voice came from somewhere in the room like a ghost, but I assumed it was some kind of speaker system. "We have intercepted a Cerberus craft and have destroyed it. Ion cannons were locked and programmed to target Outpost Nine and the High Councilor's meeting."

That was the last straw and apparently enough to prove Bertok's guilt. The guards stepped toward Bertok, ready to take him into custody or whatever they did on Trion. But he wanted nothing to do with it. He tried to run past us, to get away, which was totally futile.

Still, it gave me one last moment of fun. I swung the titan stick up in a wide arc and brought it back down, clotheslining Bertok with the weapon across his chest. His feet flew up, and he dropped onto his back like I'd been a linebacker taking him out.

I grinned down at the asshole. I wanted to zap him again, but I didn't. Then I thought of Naron and did just that, jabbed the fucker in the side with the sizzling stick. He writhed and screamed in pain. "That's for my Naron, you fucker."

"Mate, please tell me all is well there," Isaak's father said.

Eela moved to stand beside me, looked down at Bertok. "Everything is as it should be. Bertok is finished."

I looked to Eela, smiled. "Yeah, it's all over."

"Zara?" Isaak's voice came through the speakers. "Are you unharmed?"

"I'm fine, Isaak." Fine. One of the worst words in existence. Because I was so *not* okay, not with any of this.

The guards lifted Bertok to his feet and dragged him away. It was over.

Cerberus was out of Trion's airspace, their attempt to get revenge on Bertok failed. I had to assume the Rogue 5 leader would be content in knowing Bertok would be in jail for the rest of his life and would have no more issues with the planet. Or with me.

One more reason to get the hell out of here as fast as humanly possible. Reason one? Save myself any future trouble with Cerberus. Reason two? Hide my broken heart. I wasn't sure which was worse.

Isaak would head back to space. His help was no longer needed. I was free. Able to do whatever I wanted. Isaak wanted to go back to space, to his hunting and running.

His pain was his to deal with. I couldn't heal him. I couldn't save him. And I couldn't convince him that he had a home.

And like it or not, I did too. On Earth. No one said I had to go back to Boston. Maybe I'd find a nice beach somewhere and mind my own damn business. Peace was finally mine, and I would hold onto it.

I was free, but why was I so sad?

One of the Councilors approached me. I bit back a shocked gasp when he kneeled at my feet. "My lady, I am Barron. Your mate, Naron, was my cousin."

"I'm so sorry." I had no idea what else to say. This Barron was handsome, young, but not as young as Naron had been. But then, Naron had been a guard, and this male was a Councilor.

"Do not apologize. Today you have delivered justice for Naron's murder, saved every member of the High Council, and saved this city from Cerberus."

Well, when he put it that way... "It wasn't just me. I had help from Isaak and his family."

"Ah, High Councilor Henrick and his surviving son."

"Yes. And Eela." Isaak's mother had moved to stand beside me, but she was watching, a strange look in her eye I couldn't quite figure out. Was this making her happy? Sad? Angry? And what was this, exactly? Why was a Councilor from Trion, an alien I'd never met before, kneeling at my feet?

"Lady Zara, you are brave, intelligent and very beautiful. I would be honored to accept you into my home and offer my protection."

Oh.

"Your protection?"

He reached for my hand and brought it to his lips. "Yes, and my devotion to your personal well-being and happiness."

Oh! Shit. Was this guy asking to be my mate? My new Trion mate? What was I supposed to do? Give him a test run? Just say yes? Say no? I had no idea how to react when the bottom line for me was I didn't want him. My heart and soul already belonged to someone else. Someone who didn't want a mate. "You are very kind, but--"

"Back away from my mate, Barron."

Barron didn't break eye contact with me not for one second. It was like Isaak wasn't even there, speaking his nonsense. "*Gara,* you will be honored and protected as my mate. I will adorn you properly and, as your master, see to your every desire." He kissed the back of my hand again, his lips lingering this time. "Your every pleasure, my lady."

Why was this guy on his knees? Why wasn't it Isaak?

Barron was handsome. Built. Earnest. I had no doubt he would do exactly as he claimed. He would take care of me, adorn me, make me have unlimited orgasms.

But I didn't want him to touch me. There was only one male from Trion I wanted, and he wasn't staying.

I pulled my hand from Barron's grip as gently as I

could. "Thank you very much for your offer, but I'm afraid I already have a master." One that didn't want me and had no intention of staying, but that was irrelevant. I'd already given my heart away, and I had no idea how I would ever get it back.

Eela took my hand, and I allowed her to pull me away. Past Barron. Past Isaak. Away. I knew we would go back to their home, and once there, I would lock myself in a room and cry until I had nothing left. And then I'd go home.

saak

EVER SINCE I first heard of a human female at Omega Dome, I'd been intrigued. Concerned. Perhaps deep down, I'd thought I would save her.

Fark.

I could see clearly now that the second I saw Zara for the first time, it was me who was being saved. Saved from a life alone. A life without a home. Without a family. Without... love.

Zara, the cranky, feisty, wild female had shown me that the life I had was as empty as the sectors of space I'd been roaming. Maybe I had been the space pirate she'd called me.

A rebel. Rogue. Wild, myself.

Untamed.

No longer. Like Zenos, I was bewitched and, *fark*,

besotted by an Earthling. The guy was so big, making an Atlan beast almost seem like a toddler, and yet Ivy had him on his knees. And he was happy to be there.

The sight of Councilor Barron on his knees, offering Zara everything I had not, gripped my heart in a panic, a level of terror I'd never felt before. Not while watching my brother die, not while hunting the Hive. Zara was my heart now. Without her, the worthless muscle in my chest would not beat.

Zara was silent on the journey back to my parents' home. I didn't argue with our destination, too concerned by the blank void behind Zara's eyes.

I held her hand, but her flesh was cold to the touch, and she did not respond to me.

I was coming apart at the seams by the time we reached my childhood home. The moment the vehicle stopped, I led Zara inside to my old bed chamber and closed the door.

As soon as the lock was in place, I turned her to face me and dropped to my knees.

"Forgive me, *gara*. I demanded you call me *master*, but I did not care for you as I should. I was selfish. A fool. I demanded everything and gave you nothing."

Her pale eyes widened, but she said nothing as my hands slid the silky material up her legs, higher and higher until it was bunched at her waist in my fists. Her pussy, pink and perfect, was directly in front of my face.

Perhaps Zenos was smarter than I ever considered.

I would get her naked and make her mine, adorn her so anyone who looked upon her would know she belonged to me, know it was my medallion on a chain dangling between her breasts.

"Zara, please, accept me as your mate, and I vow that even the gods will know that while you belong to me, *I* am the one kneeling, That I am the one to submit to your every happiness. Every desire."

"Isaak. I can't do this. I can't live on that little spaceship. I want a family. A home. I want more than you can give me."

I leaned forward, rested my head on her soft belly, breathed her in. My home. My life. My everything. "I give you everything, Zara. Everything there is. If you want to live on Earth, I will follow you. I offer my home here on Trion. If that does not suit, we can go somewhere else. Anywhere, as long as I am yours. My heart and soul are yours, *qara*. Forever."

I waited for her response, the lump in my throat too big to overcome with words. I could do nothing but wait. And hope. And pray I hadn't been too much of a fool.

When her hands lifted to my head, her fingers tunneling through my hair, I dared to breathe again.

"Master, please. You broke my heart. Convince me. Make me believe you."

Master.

She'd said the word once before, to Barron, during his attempt to steal her away from me. But I had not dared believe it. But I would deserve her trust. Shower her with love and pleasure. And that started now, leaning forward and nuzzling her clit with my nose.

She gasped, widened her stance. Glancing up at her, I smiled. She wanted it. Whatever *it* was I would give to her.

With her legs further apart, I could lick her core, lap at the arousal that was always there. For me. Her taste, as wild and sweet as the female herself, coated my tongue.

Her hand dropped onto my head, her fingers tangling in my hair. Tugging me into her. I could tease her, bring her close to her climax and retreat again and again. I could. I had. I wouldn't now.

Now it would be the opposite. I worked her with my tongue, my lips until she was panting. Gasping. Crying my name.

My cock was throbbing in my now-tight pants. My balls ached to be emptied, filling her and marking her deep in her pussy. Soon.

First, she would know that she belonged to me. That she was mine, body and soul. A Bride's testing wasn't necessary to know this. We didn't have marked palms like Everians. I didn't have seed power like the Viken males. *Fark,* I was proud I didn't need it to satisfy my mate.

When she practically ripped my hair out as she came, her desire coating my mouth, my chin, my happiness was this. Her.

Us.

When her knees gave out, I collected her into my arms, lifted and carried her to the bed. I sat on the edge, held her on my lap.

"*Gara*, it is time to make you truly mine," I murmured.

"We've already had sex," she replied, nuzzling her face into my chest.

Setting her before me on her feet, I held my hands on her hips, the dress falling back down around her ankles. I was eye level with her breasts, her nipples with the little rings and chain clearly visible through the sheer fabric.

From my shirt pocket, I pulled out the family

medallion. It had heft, but not enough to be painful for her as it would soon hang permanently from the chain between the rings.

"Mated Trion females are adorned. I've mentioned this before, but it has never been the right time. Now, it is." I held the medallion between two fingers, so she could see it. "This is my family crest. It would make me proud if you wore it."

"Where?" she asked, her voice skeptical.

With one slow finger, I slid the strap of her dress off one shoulder then did the same with the other, so they were caught in the crook of her elbows. Her breasts were bare. Perfect. The pink nipples hardening as I watched.

Leaning forward, I licked one, flicked the hoop with my tongue. "Here." I moved to the other nipple, gave it equal attention. "And here." The chain swung slightly from the action.

She gasped but remained silent. "I will add jewels to the rings. Matching ones to this little Earth adornment." I nudged the piercing in her navel. I glanced up at her. "I want to add a ring to your clit, bejewel it."

She squirmed at my words. The idea of it made her hot. The reality of it would make her even hotter.

"Yes. Now. Please."

My eyes widened in surprise. I was expecting her to argue, to offer up some kind of rebellion for the submission that wearing my adornments would permanently bring.

Her arms straightened by her sides, the dress sliding silently down her body to pool around her ankles. Her hands went to her pussy, her fingers bracketing her hardened clit. It poked out at me, swollen and eager for more attention. "Do it. God, the idea of a ring here makes me want to come again. I had no idea it would, but I want it with you."

I had to know the reasons for her interest in it. She was aroused now, and I would not have her decision based on swirling desire. She needed to be clear headed enough to understand what it meant.

"Why?" I asked.

She arched a pale brow. "Because I love you, you idiot. I want to be yours. Permanently. I tested to Trion for a reason. I will submit but only to you. I'm proud to be yours. I want you to see my body and know it belongs to you."

She'd said so much, but I was snagged on three specific words. "You love me?"

Rolling her eyes, she laughed. "Yes. I have no idea why since you're such a stubborn, bossy—"

I didn't let her say more only pulled her in for a kiss. She loved me!

I claimed her with my mouth, reveling in the feel of her in my arms, in the knowledge that she was mine, not just in body, but heart and soul.

"I love you, Zara," I clarified.

"It's *gara,*" she countered, completely at odds with every stubborn rebuttal she'd ever made.

I couldn't help but grin. "That's right, you're mine."

"Yes."

"And you want my adornments? Even a clit ring? There will be no question you belong to me."

"Who's going to see my clit?" she wondered.

"Me," I growled. A traditional Trion custom was to have a claiming witnessed by others.

That wasn't going to happen with us. No chance. Zara was mine and *only* mine.

"Still... I... I want it. For you."

I loved those words from her lips, but they weren't completely accurate.

"You have to want it for you. To see it. Feel it and know you are loved, that you belong to someone. That I belong to you enough to have your clit claimed and adorned for me."

She ran a finger over my shoulder as she thought. "I understand. It's still a yes."

So many feelings coursed through me. I was... happy. I knew I had to make my own happiness, but I'd found it in Zara. I wasn't going to wait for her to change her mind not that it seemed as if she would. I gripped her hips and stood, turned us around, so she could sit on the edge of the bed where I had just been.

"Not until you ask me properly."

She frowned. While her admitting her love was a balm to my wounded soul, it wasn't what I wanted from her. What I'd commanded from her all along.

I waited patiently as she figured it out. As I watched her mind work through it.

She licked her lips. Said the one word I'd been dying to hear from her lips.

"Master."

I groaned, closed my eyes.

"Master, please adorn me. Make me yours in every way."

Taking a moment, I savored her words. The almost begging sound of her voice. Her need.

I lifted my lids, studied the female before me. She

meant it. I could see it in the relaxed lines of her gorgeous body, of the need in her gaze. In the love I saw there.

"Wait," I commanded.

"Yes, Master."

I went to the bathing room, opened a drawer and pulled out the items I would need for this claiming. It *would* be a claiming. Now that I was her master, she would be mine in all ways. I would ensure everyone knew that. I'd never imagined the rings and piercing tools within would ever be used. I'd walked away from the possibility of a Trion mate at the same time as I had my family. My planet.

I returned with everything I needed, set them on the bed beside her. Leaning down, I kissed her upturned lips. Just as sweet as her lower ones.

"This will not hurt," I murmured when I finally lifted my head.

She made a funny sound. A scoff. "Um, you're going to pierce my clit hood. I think it's going to hurt. A lot."

I shook my head. "Trust me?"

She nodded, her pale hair sliding over her shoulders. "Yes, Master."

Fark, I'd never tire of hearing that.

"Good. Lie down. Feet on the edge of the bed. Good girl. Wider. Even wider."

When she finished complying with my directions, she was bare and on her back, her pussy on display with her knees splayed open.

Picking up the piercing tool, I prepared the small ring to it, I carefully set it over her clit, so it was tucked beneath the hood. I'd never done this before, but all Trion males learned of these skills upon becoming a man. For just such a moment. When the ring was in place, I grabbed the ReGen wand, turned it on and set it right beside her clit as I activated the piercer.

It was over from one second to the next, and I tossed the tool aside, kept the healing wand in place, just in case.

Zara gasped, but she hadn't even flinched. Coming up on her elbows, she looked down her body at her new adornment. The tiny blue gem that dangled from it the same color as her eyes.

"It's done?"

"Did it hurt?"

She shook her head, and I tossed the wand away.

Staring at it in wonder, she put her fingers on it, flicked the metal. Gasped again.

Fark, I was going to come in my pants at the sight of her. I wanted to flick it with my tongue, make her come again. But I wasn't done.

Taking her hand, I helped her sit up. Once again, I dropped to my knees before her. Grabbing the medallion again, I attached it to the center of the chain. Her head was bent as she watched, then when it was attached, I moved her shoulders from side to side to make the chain sway.

"*Fark,*" I swore. "So beautiful."

Her head lifted, her eyes met mine. She was crying.

"You are hurting?" I asked, panicked.

She shook her head. "Happy."

I sighed.

"Horny. God, how am I going to walk?"

I couldn't help but grin. "Constantly aroused. And wet."

"Mmm, let me find out."

I dropped to my knees again, got my mouth on her. At first, I was careful with the new ring, flicking it gently to test her response. She gasped and gripped the bedding. She was so wet, there was too much to lap up. I didn't even try, only played with her new adornment until she came—which was obscenely swift. Yes, the clit ring was going to be such fun.

I stood once again, set my hands on my hips, took in my sated mate. My cock wept with pre-cum at my skill to satisfy my mate.

"Holy crap, that was intense. On Earth, we get a ring on our finger." She held up her left hand and waved it about.

"Not very exciting," I replied.

"This is definitely better," she said, her voice all breathy. Her skin shone in the light like a pearl with a bloom of sweat.

"So much."

"I wonder what sex is like with it," she said, curious. Ah, my mate was insatiable. That pleased me so.

As I stripped off my clothes, I said, "Let's find out."

———

Zara

Isaak was gorgeous. I knew guys didn't like to be called that, but as I watched him take off his clothes to stand before me bare, cock long and thick thrusting out from the juncture of his thighs, I couldn't believe he was mine.

All mine. I felt the warm weight of his medallions against my chest. I couldn't feel the clit ring. It had been as he'd said. No pain. No healing. That ReGen wand was insane. I moved, so I was on my knees on the bed. The action made the dangling chain sway, the clit ring shift. Oh my God. I hoped I got used to them because I had a feeling I was going to be constantly aroused. Sure, the way Isaak's gaze flared with heat at the sight of his adornments meant he loved seeing me marked as his. But it wasn't a one-way arrangement. I got pleasure from them too. Every time I moved, I'd know Isaak was mine, that he would only bring me happiness and pleasure.

Starting now. We were on Trion to stay. His parents... well, that was improved, but it would take time for them to work through all of their issues. He had a family. He had me. I had a new planet. A mate. A life. Love.

Isaak gripped his cock at the base, stroked it a few times from root to tip then moved to kneel on the bed with me. My pussy clenched with the need for him to be inside me. He wasn't moving fast enough, so I pressed my body to his. He sat back on his heels which gave me room to climb in his lap, nestling the head of his cock at my entrance. Our eyes were almost aligned. I watched him as I lowered myself, taking him into me an inch at a time.

His hand came to my butt and helped, pushing me down, but I was so aroused that he filled me with ease.

I sighed. He hissed. I clenched around him, adjusting. The clit ring brushed against the base of his shaft, the sensation new. Intense.

"God, you feel so good," I said.

"*Gara,*" he groaned.

"So good, Master."

Yes, he was that to me. My everything.

Between one heartbeat and the next, Isaak lifted me up and off him, spun me about, so I faced away from him on all fours, then plunged deep. The chain dangled toward the bed and swayed with every hard thrust.

"Master!" I cried. How did he know I wanted it hard? Fast. Deep. It was insane how incredible it was between us.

A hand wound about my waist and pulled me back, so I was once again straddling his thighs, but now facing away from him. The hand lifted to my breast, cupped it and plucked at the nipple ring. The other slid between my thighs and played with the newest adornment. His hips thrust up and took me deep as he pushed me to come.

It didn't take much. My clit was so sensitive with the ring, almost too much. But that was the love I felt for him. It was so intense it was almost too much.

I cried out as I came, Isaak taking me hard once, twice, then calling out my name as he came too.

I loved him. The need for him would be almost painful with the intensity of it. I'd volunteered to be in space for a mate. For a match. A master.

This went deeper, like his cock. I didn't know where he ended and I began.

This was it for me. Isaak was it. I'd never get enough. Never doubt his love, his desire. I was marked. I was his. And he was mine. My rebel mate.

A SPECIAL THANK YOU TO MY READERS...

Want more? I've got *hidden* bonus content on my web site *exclusively* for those on my mailing list.

If you are already on my email list, you don't need to do a thing! Simply scroll to the bottom of my newsletter emails and click on the *super-secret* link.

Not a member? What are you waiting for? In addition to ALL of my bonus content (great new stuff will be added regularly) you will be the first to hear about my newest release the second it hits the stores—AND you will get a free book as a special welcome gift.

Sign up now! http://freescifiromance.com

FIND YOUR INTERSTELLAR MATCH!

YOUR mate is out there. Take the test today and discover your perfect match. Are you ready for a sexy alien mate (or two)?

VOLUNTEER NOW!

interstellarbridesprogram.com

DO YOU LOVE AUDIOBOOKS?

Grace Goodwin's books are now available as audiobooks...everywhere.

LET'S TALK!

Interested in joining my **Sci-Fi Squad**? Meet new like-minded sci-fi romance fanatics and chat with Grace! Get excerpts, cover reveals and sneak peeks before anyone else. Be part of a private Facebook group that shares pictures and fun news! Join here:

https://www.facebook.com/groups/scifisquad/

Want to talk about Grace Goodwin books with others? Join the **SPOILER ROOM** and spoil away! Your GG BFFs are waiting! (And so is Grace) Join here:

https://www.facebook.com/groups/ggspoilerroom/

GET A FREE BOOK!

JOIN MY MAILING LIST TO BE THE FIRST TO KNOW OF NEW RELEASES, FREE BOOKS, SPECIAL PRICES AND OTHER AUTHOR GIVEAWAYS.

http://freescifiromance.com

ALSO BY GRACE GOODWIN

Interstellar Brides® Program: The Beasts

Bachelor Beast

Interstellar Brides® Program

Assigned a Mate

Mated to the Warriors

Claimed by Her Mates

Taken by Her Mates

Mated to the Beast

Mastered by Her Mates

Tamed by the Beast

Mated to the Vikens

Her Mate's Secret Baby

Mating Fever

Her Viken Mates

Fighting For Their Mate

Her Rogue Mates

Claimed By The Vikens

The Commanders' Mate

Matched and Mated

Hunted

Viken Command

The Rebel and the Rogue

Ascension Saga, book 5

Ascension Saga, book 6

Faith: Ascension Saga - Volume 2

Ascension Saga, book 7

Ascension Saga, book 8

Ascension Saga, book 9

Destiny: Ascension Saga - Volume 3

Other Books

Their Conquered Bride

Wild Wolf Claiming: A Howl's Romance

ABOUT GRACE

Grace Goodwin is a USA Today and international bestselling author of Sci-Fi and Paranormal romance with more than one million books sold. Grace's titles are available worldwide in multiple languages in ebook, print and audio formats. Two best friends, one left-brained, the other right-brained, make up the award winning writing duo that is Grace Goodwin. They are both mothers, escape room enthusiasts, avid readers and intrepid defenders of their preferred beverages. (There may or may not be an ongoing tea vs. coffee war occurring during their daily communications.) Grace loves to hear from readers! All of Grace's books can be read as sexy, stand-alone adventures. But be careful, she likes her heroes hot and her love scenes hotter. You have been warned...

www.gracegoodwin.com
gracegoodwinauthor@gmail.com

Printed in Great Britain
by Amazon